• • •

THE FAKE REALITY PRESIDENT

D0967728

Thanks

THE FAKE REALITY PRESIDENT

The Conspiracy to Steal the U.S. Government

CHARLES K. SPETZ

© 2017 Charles K. Spetz
All rights reserved.

ISBN-13: 9781974035311
ISBN-10: 197403531X
Library of Congress Control Number: 2017911964
CreateSpace Independent Publishing Platform
North Charleston, South Carolina

FOREWORD

I come from a background of observing, analyzing, and questioning current events through several decades. Eight years of apparent political maneuvering by a secret cabal have been efficient and disciplined. In less than a decade, we've observed the rise of an angry-victim mindset minority hustled lockstep into unwavering support of a modern would-be autocrat following the Hitler game plan, with backing or direction from the Russian dictator. A well-planned coup has been progressing on schedule, unabated and unchallenged.

The exposure to an easily manipulated fan base for years of a fake reality-television character who is the last word on all things, the decider who may not be questioned, has transformed the election process into a sideshow—the world's longest-running twenty-four-seven fake reality-TV show. When brainwashed true believers join a Congress controlled by large corporate and private donations, the will of the majority is easily subverted. The undisputed "last word" TV character with massive media coverage challenges the president's citizenship with no credible basis for years and fuels the nation's racist elements.

This persistent effort to delegitimize the president, combined with the Republican Congress's adoption of a treasonous goal of "making this president fail" has divided the electorate and paved the way for hacking and Russian interference in our democratic process. This long-running attack on our nation and values is concealed by nonstop media manipulation and one outrageous statement after another, each blatant lie overshadowed by the next with no time for reflection or discussion.

Seeing this strategy for what it is, I became alarmed that this agenda was progressing unchecked. With this realization, I wondered what I could do that might contribute to public awareness and help thwart the planned coup. The conspirators would replace our democracy with an autocratic royal crime family that would work for more control and self-enrichment at the expense of all others. I could not fathom how what seemed obvious and blatant was lost among the distractions and diversions. I realized that I could not remain passive and silently accept this theft of our democracy.

After much reflection and excellent advice, I decided that writing this serious message within a fictional thriller format could be the best path to a wider awareness of the threat we are facing and the preservation of our basic values. Following events while writing has made me realize the urgency of the threat. I knew that I must do my small part and tell this story or accept that I was not doing what I could for my country. Therefore, I have penned *The Fake Reality President* as a patriot and believer in the democratic process.

TABLE OF CONTENTS

Chapter 1

● ● ●

DISCOVERY AND CHASE

The writer was happily dozing on the sun deck on a balmy June day in Portland, Oregon, when the phone rang. It was his buddy Nick Steele, with a wild tale to tell.

"del Mundo showed up on my dock on his tender, dropped a package on me, and said he had to turn around and head back to the research vessel off the island."

"What kind of package?"

"He said to get this to you and then get lost for a while, as he was doing. He said it was about the greatest theft in history—the theft of the government of the most powerful nation on earth. The FedEx will be there soon, and I'm going to be abroad for a while, so good luck."

Before he had hung up, the doorbell rang, and there was the FedEx package, slapped into the writer's hand, thank you very much—or not. He opened the package with anticipation and trepidation after the strange manner of its arrival. There was a leather-bound portfolio with a note attached in del Mundo's handwriting.

"We were in port in Mexico at a yacht club, slip number thirteen, taking on supplies, when this package was delivered, addressed only to the slip number. The name of the vessel intended had been washed away, and the package was quite wet. After drying out the papers and still not knowing if the delivery was to the right vessel, we opened the portfolio to determine if we were the intended recipients. Viewing the contents, it became obvious that not only was it sent to us in error but also that the previous boat in the slip had departed without the delayed delivery. It was also apparent that the information contained was highly sensitive and potentially dangerous. We felt it to be expedient to put out to sea immediately to elude the tracers who were sure to be tasked with recovering the documents. Having been chased through time zones and latitudes, we finally found a storm to hide in and slip this to Nick on his island and continue the ruse of running to give Nick some slack to pass it on to you. You are unknown for now, but there is no guarantee how long this condition will last. When you have read this, you will understand the seriousness and the determination spurring this hunt. This word must get out to the American people before it is too late. I have faith in you and wish you success, for all our sakes."

With this ominous message, he opened the folder:

A. Assembly of secret cabal
  1. Create strategy and create time line
  2. Define and acquire needed required personnel

3. Launch probes
   a. Make blatant false statements to gauge gullibility of public
   b. Make racial slurs to determine public racial biases and fearfulness
   c. Attack leaders to undermine legitimacy (birther untruth)
4. Make support agreement with Russian president
   a. Hacking and release of opponent's e-mails
   b. Use of disinformation team

B. Announce run for president
   1. Gauge polls, reactions
   2. Identify areas of resonance and objections
C. Announce not running
D. Begin media manipulation
   1. Create TV show with candidate as all-powerful character, the last word (no dissent possible, no balance, character's word is final)
   2. Begin use of dog whistle–like key words
      a. Candidate tough, strong, only one who can save us
      b. Others weak, dumb, crooked
   3. Begin use of separating language
      a. "Us or them" themes
      b. Quantify reactions and responses
E. Announce real run in upcoming election
   1. Stage announcement at candidate-owned property
   2. Use casting call for paid extras to wear hats and T-shirts and cheer

F. Develop no-cost media strategy
  1. Make outrageous statements, true or false
  2. If statements are challenged or fact-checked, repeat, stretch story
  3. Play to fears and when news cycle slows, release next fantasy
  4. Prejudices, truth unimportant, massive airtime as goal
G. Transference
  1. Accuse others of doing what candidate is doing
H. Manipulation
  1. Repeat conditioning words
    a. In all honesty, to be honest, frankly, to be frank, believe me, trust me, I am only one who knows, I am the best, take it from me, etc.
I. Stage campaign events
  1. Rallies at candidate-owned properties, creating personal income
    a. Pay actors to carry signs and cheer
    b. Demonize all "others," blacks, Muslims, Hispanics, gays, socialists, Democrats
    c. Encourage violence
    d. Attack and disparage objective media to delegitimize, accuse of bias
    e. Deny press credentials for questioning reporters
    f. Attack judicial system
    g. Promise tax cuts for wealthiest

 h. Promise tax cuts for corporations
 i. Promise removal of restrictions on Wall Street
 j. Promise to destroy labor unions
 k. Intimidate party leaders
 l. Continue impossible ideas like a wall and deportation of eleven million immigrants

Strategy: Candidate is strong, has secret data no one else has. Avoid debates, use controlled events only. Answer no questions directly. Respond with distractions, talk down president. Use diversions. Repeat, repeat, repeat. Brainwash with mixture of fear and hate. With enough repetitions of false statements, truth becomes irrelevant in people's minds.

J. Secure nomination
 1. Continue and increase all outrageous statements
 2. Continue attacks on all "others"
 3. Recruit militia groups, organize private security force
 4. Increase attacks on "crooked media"
 5. Launch Russian hacking efforts
 6. Research vote-counting systems for vulnerable points and bribable employees
 7. Initiate clandestine funding for progressive independent third-party candidate to split Democratic vote

Strategy: With use of Russian hacking and media manipulation using trolls and bots to blanket social media news with huge downloads of false stories, and an October surprise, election result is guaranteed.

K. Aftermath
  1. Nationalize major industries
  2. Build more private prisons and detention centers
      a. Profit source owned by candidate and associates
  3. Incarcerate vocal dissenters, illegal immigrants, and enemies of candidate
  4. Siphon funds from trade deals and government contracts
  5. Complete redistricting of country
  6. Increase obstacles to minority voting
  7. Repeal Affordable Care Act, create health care system to profit insider group while cutting services
  8. Privatize Social Security

The candidate has decided that the job of a czar has a better pay plan than that of president. He is counting on the combination of fear, racial biases, and greed, coupled with the low information of the general public, to allow this sinister plan to succeed. With the right timing combined with Russian assistance, this country may wake up to find itself under authoritarian rule, its democracy stolen. In a blink, we will find ourselves in a hell that is difficult to escape.

Chapter 2

●　　●　　●

PROBE FOR A VOICE

The writer was Kent Steiger, an English major, who wrote proposals, advertising material, magazine and newspaper articles, and the occasional short story. Between these works, there had been occasional special projects like the ones with Nick and del Mundo. The likes of del Mundo and Nick were rare and honorable. Each, in his own way, had proved to be unscrupulously honest and especially considerate of others.

While reviewing the agenda outlined in the package, Steiger found the slightly fantastical script playing out in real life. The name-calling of primary opponents and vulgarity were becoming so regular that the media could not keep up. In the needed time for any reflection, clarification, or reaction to be heard, the next absurdity was in the news. The false reality-TV world was moving at a much faster pace than any sober discussion. The practicality or truthfulness of any statements or promises were lost in the next Twitter post. The so-called crooked media, while being demonized, were slavishly reporting every statement and driving coverage at no cost to the campaign.

Through this blanket of noise, he needed to locate a media-qualified reliable ear—an uncompromised ally.

Aware that Nick was still "getting lost" around the globe, he made a call to a reporter in Seattle who he had said was trustworthy.

When Richard Douglas answered the phone, there were multiple media soundtracks in the background.

"Hi, Richard, you don't know me, but our mutual friend, Nick Steele, said you could be trusted, and I need assistance with some sensitive material."

"OK," he said. "I have heard Nick mention your name in a good way. What's up?"

"This material involves a serious national threat that is timely, and I feel it best to discuss in person."

"That sounds ominous and important."

"If you consider a threat to the existence of our democracy significant, then, yes, it is both. Being that there is great urgency involved, I could travel to you if you have any time."

"That sounds like there is a risk of danger. As Nick spoke highly of you, I can certainly make time. My weekend is booked, but next week would work."

"Thank you. Then I will head your way Monday if that is good."

"Let's say lunch to afford you travel time. Call me when you are moving, and we'll set the meeting place."

"Thank you. Looking forward to Monday."

After hanging up, Steiger did a little background research to have a better picture of Nick's friend and their possible ally.

He knew Richard had written a few pieces way back for *Rolling Stone*, some exposés, but was surprised to learn that he had spent time in Iraq during the US invasion and occupation. He specifically criticized the false excuse for invading, based on weapons of mass destruction, as well as the massive no-bid corporate contracts. Add in accounts of the missing 747 loads of hundred-dollar bills, and he was gaining street cred and earning places on political enemies' lists. Lately, he had been covering mostly noncontroversial stories for the *Seattle Times*, staying well under the radar.

As Steiger began to understand Richard's connection to Nick, he felt this meeting could be productive but realized the mission could prove too great a threat to his low-key life.

He needed some help with a media contact right away but couldn't fault Richard if the whole thing was too risky for him. He would need to make his own choice.

While he prepared for the trip, packing the agenda in his metal briefcase, the sideshow media blitz was increasing in volume and accelerating from grade school name-calling to reckless ideas: a border wall paid for by Mexico, the deportation of eleven million undocumented immigrants, a ban on Muslims entering the United States, and so forth. At the same time, the media were providing millions of dollars' worth of coverage for free. The rapid-fire messages were delivered to cheering crowds at pep rallies of supporters, with many casting call paid extras, seemingly oblivious to the unreality or unconstitutional nature of it all. The name-calling and "us versus them" sermonizing was giving voice to disdained radical fringe groups and creating a hateful, violent climate.

With the size and fervor of these events increasing, he drove north with a palpable feeling of danger.

Heavy traffic made the drive slow, so he was a little worn down approaching Seattle and calling Richard, who suggested Ivar's for clam chowder and halibut, which sounded like good fortification, which would definitely be needed. A tall, lanky guy with dark curly hair and thick black-framed glasses, Richard was easy to spot as he walked in, though he had more gray hair than in his old pictures. He was sitting at the bar, sipping a beer and watching the door.

"Richard," Steiger said, "good to meet you. Sorry to make you wait. Traffic was bad."

"No problem. I've not been here long. Welcome to Seattle," he said, getting up for a handshake. "It's nice to meet you also, and you've definitely triggered my imagination with your phone call."

"This is probably even wilder than you may have imagined. Can we find a private booth?"

"We can do that," Richard said, eying the metal briefcase. After settling into a quiet corner, Steiger filled him in on the delivery of the package, and Richard was obviously nervous. They paused as the waitress took lunch orders. When she left, he pulled out the document and passed it to Richard, who scanned the package, grew visibly disturbed, and placed it out of sight under his jacket as lunch was delivered. As they munched and sipped, Steiger could see his mind working behind the glasses.

"If this was from any source other than del Mundo, I would immediately dismiss it as another wacky conspiracy theory," he said quietly. "By the way, where are del Mundo and Nick?"

Steiger filled him in on del Mundo's pursuit and evasive decoying maneuvers and Nick's multi-continent air journey to get off the grid.

"This is certainly larger and worse than I expected or wanted," Richard said.

"As a patriot, I cannot turn my back on it, but the method of exposing and thwarting this plan will be tricky and probably dangerous. I could certainly use your help, if the jeopardy for you is not too prohibitive," said Steiger.

Although Richard had written about some highly charged events over the years and had much credibility and a reputation for fearlessness, this was another level. "There is great danger here, including substantial forces that would be capable of extreme means to suppress this information," he said in a somber tone. "But with the stakes being so high and the planned consequences so enormously wrong, I would always have a difficult time looking in the mirror if I turned my back. Yes, for you, del Mundo, Nick, myself, and our nation, I must join the team to prevent the theft of our democracy."

"I figured Nick was right about you."

"We must be extremely careful and find a way to locate and involve the right people with the power and ability to help expose and foil this unconscionable plan. Can you remain in Seattle so we can gather data, identify potential uncompromised allies, and formulate a strategy?"

"Yes, I can, and we must."

Richard was growing heated. "I have been following campaign news reports that have been discouraging and nonsensical, but goddamn it, now I see what the bastards have been up to. Goddamn. Yeah, 'We've got to build a wall, keep out the Muslims, lock up Mildred,' and the swastika crowd at the rallies goes wild."

Richard said he had a guest cottage where Steiger would be comfortable on his secluded property and suggested they head to his home to be unseen and safe, though he had no indication that Nick's del Mundo contact had been detected.

"Sounds good if you are sure it is not too much of an imposition and your wife is on board. We definitely need to find secure access to media, and quickly."

As they drove to Richard's house, Steiger wondered how del Mundo was faring and when Nick would be back in the picture. Although grateful for Richard's help, he fretted that the plan might be too far along and that it may be too late to prevent the unthinkable.

Richard's home on a wooded hillside near Edmonds was situated in a park-like setting with views over Puget Sound. The main house was a two-story log structure with wings, high ceilings, and generous decks. Inside were big logs, hardwood floors, large windows, and multiple stone fireplaces. Down a short path in a copse of fir was a smaller cottage, also of log construction. This was the cozy guesthouse where Steiger would be quartered for now.

Richard and his wife, Jan—a tall, attractive blonde—had been married for thirty-plus years, with two grown daughters raised and gone, beginning families of their own. When she and Steiger were introduced, she was warm and said that since he was not there to drag Richard off to the Middle East again, he was to feel welcome. After a glass of wine and a light dinner and agreeing that Richard could bring Jan into the loop of the mission, the subject of Nick came up.

Steiger told them how he and Nick had traveled in the same circles for a time, bumping into each other at events and skiing at various locations. Sometimes at parties they found themselves interested in the same women. With Nick's chiseled build over six feet, Steiger was lucky he had a low-key demeanor and was considerate of others, so there were never any troubles between them. He didn't know much then about Nick's background, only that he had served in the military, and over time they became friends. He was always honest and humble, and he introduced Steiger to del Mundo at an Aspen Institute conference one year.

Professor del Mundo was a slight, tidy man with a perpetual quizzical smile, shaggy gray hair, and wire-rimmed glasses. When they met, he was wearing pressed khakis, a blue dress shirt, a lightweight dark-blue blazer, and brown tassel loafers. He was soft-spoken, with twinkling bright-blue eyes and an obvious good humor. He was a scientist who lived on his research vessel in whatever locations his projects took him, his whereabouts frequently difficult to determine. He was associated with a think tank–like secret committee of patriots who had remained unknown since the 1800s while performing many off-the-books missions around the globe to protect our democracy.

Del Mundo had enlisted Nick in several of these actions over the years in different countries and domestically that had prevented great harm and remain classified and unknown. The president, or chairman, of this secret group had been impressed with Nick's skills and courage. The respect was mutual, and Nick referred to him as his "rabbi." Del Mundo had had the utmost confidence of a succession of presidents and was a brilliant thinker

and seemingly well-schooled in every facet of life's challenges, yet he remained a humble, pleasant person, kind
and considerate to a fault, uplifting to be around.

Richard's story about Nick was more exciting.

"While in Iraq writing war stories, terrorists attacked
a school I was visiting. They killed several Iraqi guards
and were holding hostage a dozen girls and their young
teacher, along with my assistant and me. We didn't know
whether we would be killed or bartered or what. After
several hours of confusion, a bearded man in a Bedouin
robe and hood arrived at the stone hut we were in. He
spoke the local dialect and claimed to have orders from
the terrorists' headquarters, sowing confusion in their
captors. When he was led inside, seeing the young girls
seemed to set off a switch in him. In a blur, he overpow-
ered and killed all five terrorists with a knife and pistol.
This was over in seconds. Then very calmly, speaking in
English, he said, 'I'm Nick, and we need to get out of
here.'

"He herded us, still in shock, out of the hut and across
the dunes, stopping only to pick up one or two of the
smaller children, carrying some piggyback. After a mile
or more, we came to a Humvee hidden and covered with
camouflage netting. Piling in, we crossed the rugged terrain for miles and made it to a US Army outpost, where
we were safe. He said he couldn't abide anyone who would
harm children. We exchanged information, and he said
he must go and asked only that I keep him out of my

story. We have had occasional contact here in the States, always pleasant. I figure that I owe him my life, as do the schoolgirls. I have often wondered where he is from, grew up, went to school, that kind of stuff."

"I have learned about Nick in pieces, over several drinking-buddy talks," Steiger began. "I can fill in some things for you. He speaks well of you, so I doubt he would mind my sharing a story, but you would probably be well advised to not repeat it or mention it to him. His family had a small farm in southern Ohio, just across the river from Kentucky. He has a brother and sister, twins two years younger than him. His father, Jack, was a veteran US Marine Corps captain who served in Vietnam and received two Purple Hearts and commendations for bravery. After discharge, he came back to his farm and family, scarred but not broken. They were a close-knit clan, friendly and well liked, always polite and well mannered. The kids were all athletic. Nick and his brother, Johnny, excelled at the big-three sports, and Chloe, their sister, started tennis very young and played constantly on the two courts in the little farm town. Theirs was a good life in most ways until Jack began having difficulties with depression, anxiety, and PTSD flashbacks from the war. His symptoms, when diagnosed by the family doctor, his wife Sally's uncle, were attributed to Agent Orange, which he was exposed to on missions in Vietnam. Since our government had never admitted using this chemical, the VA offered no treatment, leaving Jack and others on his team pretty much on their own. A rare cancer developed, and Jack went downhill fast and eventually died, leaving Nick the man of the house at thirteen.

"Nick used the good things he had learned from his father and grew up fast. He became the chief protector of his mom and younger siblings, determined to keep the farm going, working after school and weekends at the chores he had known all his life. A late bloomer, Nick was small for his age, though athletic with the strength of a much bigger person and a mental toughness that was off the chart. His dad had taught him martial arts and self-defense from a young age, and he was an apt pupil. He was also taught to avoid conflict if possible and if not, to end it quickly. He had also learned to be humble and considerate of others—a protector, not an assailant.

"There were several instances when he needed to protect his siblings. One of these times occurred when a group of bullies at the high school had focused on his brother and sister, ganging up and knocking them around for laughs. Both came home bruised, Johnny with a black eye and bloody nose. The easygoing Nick went ballistic after hearing that the gang followed them from school and caught them in a wooded area on their walk to the farm. Off the school grounds, there would be no help from school authorities. If asked, the bullies would deny everything and go unpunished, sure to escalate their assaults. Nick didn't even want to think what would eventually happen to Chloe and Johnny.

"The next day, Nick got an excused early leave from school for farm work and hurried home to prepare. He dug out an old belt of his father's with a heavy metal buckle. In the barn, he found a scrap of rubber hose, cut off a foot-long piece, and filled it with lead buckshot. He sealed the ends with hose clamps and duct-taped the whole thing with several tight wraps. He then went to the wooded area where the bullies had caught up with the kids. He had told Johnny and Chloe that morning to taunt the gang and then, when they were followed again, to run into the woods and hide. Sure enough, the bullies followed the kids into the woods. In a small clearing, they found Nick alone.

"'Looking for someone?' Nick asked the four larger teenagers.

"'We'll mess you up too,' said the leader, a big boy who outweighed Nick by a good sixty pounds. As he came close, Nick dodged a wild punch, sidestepped, and hit the bully in the face with the heavy hose, which flattened his nose and spewed blood. The bully dropped into a heap, eyes rolling and out cold. The next two then came at him. With the belt rolled around his other hand, Nick stopped one with a quick strike to the face, and a side kick to the knee had the other one hobbled on the ground, crying. As the last one slowed his charge, Nick caught him on the side of the head with the hose, and he too went down, not moving. Nick went to the one he had slowed down with the belt and hit him with a left hook to the jaw that stopped him. He told the one who was still conscious that if they ever came at him or his family again, he would hunt them down and kill them.

"He then caught up with Chloe and Johnny, and they all went home, where Nick continued his farm work and would swear, if ever asked, that he had been working in the field all afternoon. After scrubbing the blood off the buckle, he put the belt back into his father's old trunk and hid the hose in the barn. The only remorse he felt was for the stupidity that had them thinking it made sense to gang up on smaller kids, especially a girl.

"After graduation, Nick enrolled at Ohio University, going back to the farm on weekends and school vacations to look after the farm and his family. After high school, Chloe went to Ohio State on a tennis scholarship, and Johnny began college online while working the farm. Nick finished his degree and ROTC program and, to no one's surprise, followed his father's footsteps into the Marine Corps.

"He was accepted into the Special Operations Command, where he learned many skills, grew into his large size, and became even more lethal. He had developed a strong sense of duty to protect others and defend his country. He carried an edge and a need to improve the military so the wounded warriors would receive the treatments they had earned. I realize that is a long story, but that is an insight into some of the influences that have made Nick the guy we appreciate and respect."

They said good night, and Steiger was off to the guest-house for a good sleep and an early start. After settling into the comfy bed with its down comforter and a small blaze in the fireplace, his mind was racing. Although encouraged by Richard's choice to join the team, he had some concern that Jan might find the endeavor too dangerous for her comfort. With del Mundo and Nick also on his mind, he finally drifted to sleep, knowing that the morning would bring the urgency of research and beginning a strategy outline.

Morning began at dawn in the Douglas household with a breakfast of fresh-squeezed orange juice and omelets with mushrooms, onions, and green peppers, topped with a dab of sour cream. Alongside were generous helpings of home-fried potatoes, sausage, bacon, and bowls of fresh fruit, and, of course, strong espresso.

After they finished the meal, Richard began by bringing Steiger up to speed on his early-morning activities. First, though, he said Jan was appalled by the evil plan and was of the same patriotic mind-set as Richard regarding involvement with the team. This was a relief—not surprising, but a relief. Next, he outlined his early back-East calls.

"I spoke with two of my most trusted national TV contacts but was not encouraged with their responses. They both reported being so busy trying to keep up with the constant media nonsense noise, in addition to the name-calling and attacks on anyone at all critical of the candidate, that they sounded absolutely gun-shy. They were so wary of being targeted as 'dishonest media' that I was not comfortable sharing with them what we were sitting on. I think we need to be very cautious about any contact, as even a small whiff about the package will probably be picked up. This is a long-term, well-financed operation with widespread assets in every sector, and we do not want any ripples. These are not friendly types, and their rules of engagement are not encouraging. Any criticism at all has met with multilevel personal attacks on challengers. The suppression by intimidation is unlike anything we have previously seen in this country. This strategy is working, as candidates are dropping out almost daily."

"Do you have other contacts who might be more viable?" Steiger asked.

"Yes, but I think we first vet them for their security: Are they tight or loose? Who do they network with who may be already compromised, knowingly or not? I also feel it will be important to contact del Mundo and Nick, if possible, to develop a coordinated action plan. These folks are spooked."

"As crazy as this may sound, I agree with you," Steiger said as they headed to Richard's home office to man the single-sideband modulation unit and satellite phone for contact with the *Veritas*, del Mundo's research vessel.

Chapter 3

• • •

DECOYS FOR THE CHASE

As del Mundo was powering up the electronics, he heard Captain Dave Merrit hitting the winch, raising the anchor. Although del Mundo was deep inside the vessel, two floors below decks, the communications room had video and audio systems monitoring the entire ship. The winch whine came from the speakers, and the muffled clunk of the anchor seating, barely audible, came from the hull.

From their concealed moorage in a small inlet, they would head from Puget Sound on a course past Port Townsend north toward Vancouver, British Columbia. On the intercom, Merrit announced, "Hook is up; we are under way. We have spotted no suspicious vessels or much of anything in this fog."

"Roger that," del Mundo said. "This weather could be perfect for our upcoming costume change."

"We think we are so clever. Let's hope this ruse works. We always have plans A, B, C, D, and plan 'Oh, shit,' though we'd rather not need them."

"I expect we will be coming into satellite ranges soon if you can keep this old girl running long enough."

"We will work on it, sir, and I will join you down there shortly."

"Good, then you too can play with the screens."

"Playing" with six keyboards, twenty screens, and several computers, del Mundo began his diagram of current locations and data inputs. He had some basic information at hand instantly, to be augmented by several feeds as they came into range. He wanted the housekeeping chores completed and setups in place, enabling maximum efficiency of satellite time.

First on the housekeeping list was evasion of any chasers, leaving tracks that led only to decoy information. This dodging began with moorage space and a fuel order booked in Vancouver for three days hence. These arrangements might or might not be needed or used, depending upon the *Veritas*'s ability to remain unseen.

While satellite work would continue, the *Veritas* would anchor in a small cove near one of the many islands they would closely pass for its costume change. Lightweight composite panels would give it a fishing-boat profile with stage-set winches, spreaders, and other simulated gear. The hull colors would change to black and rusty, with new registration numbers and the name *Madeline*, a real vessel that was undergoing an unannounced decommissioning. Various audio and mechanical modifications would program and project the sonar footprint of the real *Madeline*. The programming was not time consuming, and the light weight of the costume pieces would allow the crew to make the change in a matter of a few hours.

"Crew standing by, ready for first costume change," Merrit announced as he entered the coms room.

"Good. Grab a cup and a seat. Look at these screens, powering up down the line. Any boat traffic showing up on the pilothouse radar?" del Mundo asked Merrit.

"Not yet, except for our southbound ferry, which is on schedule coming out of Vancouver, with the weather calm with thickening fog."

"Sounds perfect, like another fine adventure if the stakes did not include the world's biggest theft," said del Mundo. "We must succeed to avoid the theft of our democracy."

"It is almost unimaginable," Merrit said.

In addition to the costume change was a trawler launch fitted with more composite pieces that would augment the vessel's perceived size and radar blip. With audio programs that could be broadcast under water projecting the *Veritas*'s sonar footprint and the friendly fog, the launch would assume the *Veritas*'s identity and provide a window of misdirection that should allow the "*Madeline*" to travel unremarked.

With the southbound ferry approaching, the crew finished the final prep and the launch, as the *Veritas,* slowly continued the northern course to Vancouver and the mooring and fuel arrangements.

Next, the "*Madeline*" fell in close behind the ferry to be in the same blip. Once past Victoria, it could get lost in the fishing fleet heading out to deep water.

When the "*Madeline*" was headed out to sea, the decoy launch would divert from the Vancouver course and head south, past Victoria and out to sea, westward toward Hawaii. The service arrangements in Vancouver would be canceled "due to a change in research priorities."

As the fog held or thickened, the decoy launch moved slowly toward Vancouver and then stopped and anchored off a small island, well beyond visual range of the port, affording the "*Madeline*" time to pass Victoria and move out to get mixed up with the fishing fleet.

After a night on anchor, the launch received the coded message from the "*Madeline*"—having passed Victoria with no interference, it was heading out fishing. The launch, using the *Veritas*'s call signs and radio profile, canceled the Vancouver arrangements and headed south on the same course as the "*Madeline*," close behind that day's ferry. Once past Victoria, the launch would radio requests for docking and fuel to Honolulu and set that course.

With the switch still undetected, the "*Madeline*" was now within satellite ranges, and del Mundo was downloading intel from multiple sources—some public, some encrypted, some hacked. The data download was immense, and del Mundo was barely able to log everything and had no time yet for analyzing.

Merrit rang from the bridge. "We are well out from Victoria, with only a couple of fishing vessels in our vicinity. All proceeding normally and zero suspicious blips or radio chatter. So far, so good with the wardrobe adjustments. How are the screens looking?"

"The data download was much greater than I expected, with time only for downloading. When the satellites pass out of range, we will both need to examine the info capture, which could contain some extraordinary content."

"We will hold course steady and keep an eye out for any threatening traffic. We're moving at a steady pace through the weather and should be OK for a while," Merrit said.

"Good. I am hard at it and will buzz when we are both needed to sort it all out. Of course, please advise me of any changes in the environment on your end."

"Roger, will do."

Though the pilothouse was calm, cruising nine knots, emulating a fisherman, below decks del Mundo was frantically working to save all the downloads. As the satellites moved out of range, the data volume decreased, and he could glance at some random items. The small bits that he found a minute to scan where alarming. He was anticipating, with dread, the coming break in downloads, which would mean time for analysis.

"Hey, Dave, if all is good in the wheelhouse and our immediate environment, could you join me down here in fifteen to twenty minutes or so?"

"Roger that. Still no issues; see you in a few."

Looking over the data volume, del Mundo knew that evaluating would take a good bit of time, even with them both toiling. He was, as always, grateful for Merrit's captain skills and his keen analytical mind. He knew from experience in many complicated international operations, both above and below the radar, that today's chore gave every sign of requiring all that both could bring.

While the download was trickling to a more normal pace, the single sideband squawked with a call sign that del Mundo recognized as a long-unused, still-untraceable handle of Steiger. After responding and switching to encrypted secret frequencies, they could talk. "How are you making out?" del Mundo asked.

"Mixed progress. I have contacted, met, and enrolled Nick's trusted writer friend in Seattle, who is now an appalled and determined team member. We appear to be unnoticed by anyone and are keeping a low profile. The bad news is that the select media friends he contacted seem either laboring full time to keep up with the longest-running fake reality show or are possibly corrupted. The mood in the country is increasingly angry, vindictive, and divided. The constant crazy talk that is using all the oxygen is serving the diversionary task in the agenda more effectively than we might have imagined. Lots of thick wool covering many vulnerable eyes.

We both feel that the rapid progress of the agenda requires us to get together to strategize. The speed and transformation of the media, along with the us-versus-them divisive demonizing, are pushing the electorate closer to a surprise step off a cliff. To have any chance of stopping this scheme will take all our skills, including Nick's, whose contact we are listening for." Steiger said

"We have just completed our data download and will begin analysis within the hour. We will also begin the process on this end of contacting Nick. Based on quick scans of a few items of news data, your call for a brain trust conference seems the next necessary move. Sit tight where you are, keep your ears to the ground, and stay ready to go mobile. We will do our assessment and be back to you within hours. For now, our location is undetected and will be easily accessible, provided our actions remain unknown. Thanks, and stay tuned." Said del Mundo.

The next squawk on the single side band radio was from the new "*Veritas*. After code confirmations and switching frequencies, what prompted the call was troubling. The three-member crew—Smith, Jones, and Black (working names)—were special operations forces who would not overreact and would notice any questionable activity and keep watching. Smith said,

"We are on our course with some freighters close if we feel like mingling. We have two vessels one thousand miles or more away, one north and one south, each on an intercept course with us. They are still long range, but if their headings are deliberate, then they could prove the effectiveness of our costume change. One other coincidence could be if their footprints suggest Russian origin. We will look for your info on that."

"That is very interesting, Mr. Smith, especially in light of our recent experience. Thank you for the report. We will investigate these blips you are watching and get back to you. Keep us updated, and be ready for the next move."

"Roger, out."

"What are we looking at?" Merrit asked as he was walking in.

"Just got off radio contact with our impostor. They are still good but have spotted two potential troublemakers one thousand miles or more from them, one from north, one from south, both on possible intercept courses. They could be anything. Could we see if they have Russian footprints?" asked del Mundo.

"And we really like a coincidence, don't we?" from Merrit.

"Yes, and they can divulge patterns and can be useful when they connect to form a visible trend."

"Very true, Professor. Let's dig in."

"These possible Russian contacts are bothersome. Let's start with all data from that sector, all the leaks, rumors, activities, and stories, especially all contacts with the candidate and the candidate's businesses and associates."

"Good plan."

"You take sat A, and I'll start on B, or the reverse if you like."

"Doesn't matter. I am on it."

After an hour or more of sharp focus, certain trends were obvious to both.

"Now we know the reason for the Russian boat pursuit. This whole group of the candidate and advisers has been compromised and on Russian payrolls for a long time," said Merrit. "Some data is undocumented, but the source is a British intelligence veteran who has always been an astute, reliable ally. We are collating multiple reports from all sectors, mostly verified. The picture we are seeing is persuasive, if not 100 percent conclusive. The candidate was observed and then soon compromised by using his well-known tastes and weaknesses. When presented with the choice of personal and professional ruin or a life of personal luxury as an overpaid puppet / TV actor, his choice was automatic. This began years ago, and the package agenda is being executed flawlessly. All actions and speech should be considered through the filter of 'How does this benefit Russia?' Though well concealed by the noise and distractions, the path of the agenda is moving rapidly, obviously following the damned script. We are in far more danger than we thought, with a long-term operation well along and gaining momentum.

"There is more," said Merrit. "Hundreds of numbered offshore accounts in Switzerland, Grand Cayman, and Lichtenstein, each holding one million in US dollars. A persuasive option when seeking key endorsements and support from selected influencers who might not be easily steamrolled with some pie in the sky. 'How many have been activated and when?' are among many questions. These bribe funds are from the same source as the fees paid to actor extras to wear hats and carry signs, masquerading as supporters. All events are micromanaged in this manner to create a fake reality-TV snapshot."

As this lengthy comment from the normally taciturn Merrit was winding down, the SSB squawked.

"The vessels we have been monitoring are holding their intercept courses, have picked up speed, and are closing more rapidly—now into the 'concern' range," Smith reported.

"This is alarming, and they look like Russian boats. How soon will you be in inflatable range of the islands, and how soon will the chasers have you in range?"

"A matter of hours, not days, for both questions. It could be close."

"Stay alert, be ready to move quickly, and stay in close touch."

"Roger. We have got this."

Back to the screens, del Mundo and Merrit were closely monitoring the positions and timing of all three vessels. They had no doubt that the chasers would not hesitate to destroy the *Veritas* decoy. For the ruse to work, the decoy needed to be out to sea with no witnesses and must sink with no debris to give away the deception. They needed the chasers to fire before the crew could set off their charges so the Russians would think they did the sinking. And with this tight timing, the crew would be cutting it close to escape undetected in the inflatable and then hide near a freighter. Timing would be critical, and success was no sure thing. While this situation was playing out, signals were initiated to establish contact with Nick. The team's gathering to full strength was crucial.

Chapter 4

●　●　●

CHASERS BITE THE BAIT

On the new "*Veritas*," Smith, Jones, and Black were busy. While monitoring their radars, satellite navigation, and SSB radio, they were preparing for the rapidly approaching decoy event. Stocking the escape boat—a sixteen-foot rigid inflatable with a fifty-horsepower, four-stroke outboard motor—needed to be precise. This small craft must carry all three with personal kits, radios, and electronic gear, and, of course, the controllers and triggers for detonations. These charges would be strategically placed on the new "*Veritas*" to destroy it and sink all remnants to ensure the effectiveness of this deception. All three men had extensive training and experience with live action in multiple operations, but the need for precise timing in this unstable environment would challenge their skills. A successful outcome was in no way guaranteed, nor was their very survival. While going about their work, they received an encrypted message from del Mundo.

"Further research has determined that both chasers are of Russian origin, and additional data shows that the vessel approaching from the north is a sub hunter equipped with an array of machine guns, antiaircraft guns, depth charges, and, more significantly, guided torpedoes. The southern-approaching vessel is configured—disguised?—as a salvage vessel. The positions and speeds of both indicate that the northern-approaching one will arrive on site first, followed by the southern. This intel suggests a torpedo attack from the north, followed by a salvage effort from the south. As the torpedo boat enters firing range, the new *Veritas* should appear to take evasive action, increasing speed and showing a direction change toward the now-distant freighters. These actions should provoke a torpedo launch to prevent escape. At this point, you three must get clear in the inflatable and be ready to trigger your charges on my signal, which will be timed to the torpedo's estimated contact. Regardless of the accuracy of that shot, this timing of your detonation can achieve the desired result. You will proceed under radar, with deflectors covering an already small or nonexistent blip. You will motor to the Big Island of Hawaii and skirt the island to the harbor at Hilo. There you will be signaled and collected by our people and placed on a corporate jet for a prescheduled routine flight to Los Angeles. From the private aviation area, you will be driven by roundabout route to rejoin the *Madeline/Veritas*. Again, watch for the signal to launch in the inflatable and clear the decoy and then for the signal to detonate. The timing is critical, and we have every confidence in your ability to complete the mission. Good luck, happy sailing, and we look forward to dinner with you on *Madeline/Veritas*."

"Roger. Understood, no worries—just another average fireworks display with a little pleasure cruise over seventy-five miles of open sea in a small inflatable. Sounds like a great time. We are awaiting your signals."

With del Mundo chuckling as he closely monitored his various radars, satellite feeds, and radios, Merrit set course for San Pedro, still mingling with fishing boats and proceeding unnoticed. In San Pedro, at the end of a crowded commercial channel, there was a large warehouse with giant doors and an inside dock that could easily accommodate *Madeline/Veritas* securely out of sight. While having the appearance of another shipyard dock repair facility, the entire property and building were hardened with high-tech security equipment that would make them virtually invisible. Satellite images, radar, and sonar scans would reveal nothing, and they would still have all their electronic capabilities. All this in a run-down barn-like structure no different from scores of others in the area. *Madeline/Veritas* would time the approach to enter under cover of darkness with jamming devices providing additional stealth. First, though, would be the monitoring and scuttling of the "*Veritas*."

On the decoy, Smith, Jones, and Black were carefully packing and securing the equipment and supplies on the inflatable. They were also gingerly placing the explosives and testing all circuits and components while monitoring speeds and directions of the chasers, listening raptly for del Mundo's signal.

"We seem to have a tight window of opportunity for pulling this off," Smith said.

"We have been here before, but this does appear to be a tighter time frame than most of our other fun," Jones said. Black merely grunted.

As they were completing their tasks and preparations, the radio crackled with del Mundo's message. "Both chasers are maintaining intercept courses, still first from the north. This torpedo boat will be within firing range in the next half hour, so stand ready. In approximately fifteen minutes, with no changes occurring, we will signal you to begin apparent evasive maneuvers. When this bait is taken, we will notify you of the torpedo launch, at which time you must quickly evacuate. Are your preparations complete?"

"Roger. Ready and waiting for your signal." Smith reported.

An agonizing seventeen minutes later, the three men received the coded signal. They moved quickly from anxious waiting into swift, coordinated action, changing course and greatly increasing speed. After some quiet minutes with no perceived action, the second signal announced the expected torpedo launch. With no wasted motions, climbing into the inflatable, they motored rapidly away from the *"Veritas"* under cover of darkness and radar deflectors, which could be redundant on such a small craft. Seemingly mere seconds of tension later came the signal to detonate. Jones triggered the detonation charges, which went off at almost the same time as the torpedo's direct hit. A stunning explosion lit up the night. Although more than a mile removed by this time, a shock wave hit them, forcing a scramble to stay afloat, though some rapid bailing was needed. The timing was perfect. Both explosions as one, and the crew anticipated no telltale floating debris. Now speeding unseen toward Hawaii, they received the report from del Mundo confirming that satellite images showed no visible remains and both chasers closing in on the site in their staggered maneuver. Maintaining their speed for Hawaii, the three radioed their status to del Mundo.

On the *Madeline/Veritas*, sighs of relief and cheers broke out immediately as the word passed around to the dozen crew members. "This action went well, and let's hope it was convincing enough to stop the active searches for us for now," del Mundo said.

"Yes, but we still need to make it to the barn undiscovered, or the ruse will have been in vain," Merrit said.

"It is cloudy, soon dark, and our timing is good to slip in unnoticed. I will leave these details to you and be working in the coms room, contacting the others. We need to quickly get everyone together and organize a strategy," del Mundo said as he headed down below.

With Merrit cruising them toward the port, del Mundo worked the radio. After several coded back-and-forth messages, he was at last in contact with Nick Steele.

"I have been through Sydney, Tokyo, Hong Kong, Milan, and London, and am now headed to Mexico City," Nick said. "I thought I detected watchers on my first stops, but after some double-backs and feints, I seemed clean. Making several more moves with starts and stops, I saw nothing out of the ordinary. Changing IDs, different names, and all the standard dodges, either I got away clean or any trackers were ditched. In a few hours, I will be back in North America. What next?"

"We are all heading to the boat barn. I believe you are familiar with the place. If you catch a flight to San Diego, a car and driver will find you and give you a lift."

"Sounds good. I am still clean and will send you my flight info. Should arrive sometime tomorrow night."

After finishing with Steele, del Mundo began the same process of messages, frequency changes, and encryption to initiate with the writers. "Are you guys still secure with no indications of any notice?" del Mundo asked.

"Yes," Steiger told him. "Everything is quiet here at Richard's house with no visitors, suspicious hikers, calls, or anything else. We might be bored if not for all the outrageous statements and happenings in the campaigns, which we are closely following."

"That is encouraging," del Mundo said. "We all seem to have eluded any pursuers for now with a series of decoys and feints. Now it is important for us all to meet and plan a strategy. Nick is running clear and is en route to us. You and Richard should sweep your vehicle for any tracing devices and drive south. I will send you encrypted coordinates for your destination. You will leave your vehicle in a long-term airport parking lot and be shuttled to us by our people. Bring your notes and tapes of all related activity you have, and we will see you by tomorrow night." del Mundo broke the connection.

"That was somewhat terse but sounded better than it could have," Richard said.

"Yes, it sounds like everyone has been busy, and we can probably look forward to some interesting details. Let's get packing and get on the road after lunch. Will Jan be OK with this trip?"

"Yes, of course. You heard her say that since you were not going to drag me back to the Middle East, she had no problems. Also, from here she can monitor developments while we are on the road and advise us of any breaking events."

After a hearty lunch of homemade clam chowder, grilled salmon, baby red potatoes, and an excellent salad, they packed their gear. With a large thermos of strong Kenyan coffee, they were headed out in Richard's generic-looking SUV. In spite of emotional hugs from Jan, they left with all in fairly good spirits despite the tension on their minds.

In the inflatable, nearing Hawaii after several hours of easy cruising on smooth water, choppy currents alternating with six-foot waves reduced speed to a crawl before the Big Island was within sight. Navigating the small craft with no running lights, Smith, Jones, and Black skirted the south end of the island and turned to the harbor at Hilo. After quick flashlight codes near the entrance were exchanged, their escorts met them at a dock. They quickly unloaded and stashed the inflatable into a small boathouse and were hustled into a van headed for the private aviation area. Inside the van, they were provided with reputable business attire accompanied by sandwiches and hot coffee.

"Do we have anything medicinal for the coffee, like maybe some brandy, Irish whiskey, or something?" asked Smith.

"Only when we are cleared and wheels up." The answer was expected though encouraging.

"I love flying," Jones muttered.

Soon enough, the Boeing Business Jet was climbing rapidly with the three sailors properly fed and watered and soon sound asleep.

With del Mundo in the coms room checking data feeds from US and foreign news outlets and secure satellite reports, Merrit, timing the approach to land with the coming of a cloudy night, surveyed the entrance to the harbor. All seemed normal, with several fishing boats on the same course, but with the thickening fog visible only as radar blips. As they slowly made their way across the harbor to their channel, del Mundo came up to the bridge. "Without the aid of all this inclement weather, we might well have had a more difficult time remaining unnoticed," he said.

"Yes, this is a rare occasion when we sailors can be happy about storms and fog. There is scant boating activity, and even with this fog we should be in the nest within a half hour."

"It won't be a minute too soon; we need time together to analyze data and events to devise a strategy that catches up with this fast-moving agenda."

Soon they were sliding quietly through the channel and into the barn. The covering fog had held, and *Madeline/Veritas* was finally resting under the roof, its approach probably unseen and certainly unremarkable. They shut down the engines and switched to shore power, leaving only an emergency generator set running in case of a shore power outage. It was imperative for them to have no gaps in any com equipment with the remaining team members still on the way.

Next to arrive were Smith, Jones, and Black with their driver/escort.

"Great job. That must have been quite a ride. Glad you made it," del Mundo said.

"Yeah, it was an unusual ride, but the fireworks display made it more enjoyable," Smith said. "The flight was nice, but can we lose these monkey suits now?"

"Of course," Merrit said. "Get comfortable, grab some coffee, a meal, a nap, or whatever. We will probably be joined by the rest during the night and anticipate having a powwow in the morning to compare notes and determine our course of action."

"Aye, aye, Cap," Smith said. "Sounds good. See you tomorrow."

"Those guys are something," Merrit told del Mundo. "They make a very hazardous operation sound like a Sunday cruise, but they could have easily been killed."

"They are the best of the best and certainly know how to control their doubts, nerves, adrenaline, and everything else. Some real sick puppies."

The radio crackled to report that the writers had parked at John Wayne Airport, had been picked up, and were being driven to the barn.

"Here come the Seattle troops," del Mundo told Merrit. "Barring any unforeseen delays, they should arrive in a couple of hours."

"All we need now is to hear from Nick Steele," Merrit said.

"If his flight from Mexico City encountered no delays, he could arrive a few hours after the writers."

"Let's hope our luck and the weather keep cooperating."

"For the unfortunate situation we are in, our specific luck with the weather and other factors has so far been remarkable," del Mundo said.

Later, the writers were on board with their driver leaving.

"Nice to see you again, Kent," del Mundo said to Steiger. "It has been a long time, and I hope your surprise involvement in this matter is not too presumptive."

"I admit that the situation is extremely unsettling but must be dealt with, and I appreciate your confidence in me, although I am unsure of what actions to take or what I can do."

"Richard, it is good to have you on board also, and what you both can do is have a meal, hit your staterooms, and get some rest. We will all convene in the morning to sort out where things stand. We are anticipating Nick's arrival sometime later, so we'll be at full strength tomorrow," del Mundo said.

After the excitement of the past days, they all needed a quiet night.

Chapter 5

●　●　●

TEAM STRATEGY MEETING

The next morning, as the team gathered in the board-room / dining salon, the big surprise was Nick Steele—already munching croissants with his coffee. None of them had seen or heard him arrive.

"Hey, Nick, nice seeing you. How and when were you able to get on board with no one taking notice?" Steiger asked.

"I have been here before."

They should not have been surprised. After years of many clandestine operations with military and various intelligence agencies, his skill set certainly included sur-reptitious entry and escape. In this instance, being famil-iar with the barn, *Veritas*, and all of its systems, he could probably have gained entrance in his sleep, which might have been the case.

"It's nice that we are finally here, and we need to take a brief rest from our sailing and travel adventures and assess the situation. I trust that we've all had some rest, so let's have breakfast and then dig in," del Mundo said.

As they ate, the screens were showing network news coverage of the primary campaigns, which after their time at sea and overseas was a shocking update with one side resembling a fake reality-TV show.

After they finished the meal, del Mundo began the discussion.

"For us being forced to employ extraordinary deceptions to escape pursuers underlines the dangerous reality of this agenda. What initially may have seemed a far-fetched conspiracy with little credibility or chance of success is now revealed as a long-term, well-financed, rapidly accelerating endeavor."

The radio squawk sounded with the code for Richard's home. After the usual passwords and frequency changes, Jan reported in a halting voice, "We have some suspicious-acting hikers around the property, and the timing is disturbing, so closely following Richard's contacts with unhelpful media people."

Nick weighed in. "This in-depth follow-up of casual contacts indicates a commitment to leaving no loose ends, the work of a well-planned coup attending to all details. Successfully hidden in the constant noise of the distractions, the ease and speed of implementation is shocking and threatening. Enabling this toxic effort are the unfortunately misinformed, frightened, and thereby vulnerable American people. These conditions are the desired result of cynical calculations and disciplined application."

"With their package missing and initial retrieval actions unsuccessful, we are seeing a logical increase of activity. The same logic suggests that we will feel the same or greater level of time pressure," del Mundo said.

"I must get home," Richard said. "Jan sounds real nervous."

"Of course," said del Mundo. "I think that, for security purposes, we should have Smith drive with you. We will do some research into the people you've contacted. At this point, we need all data of any players and connections. There could be valuable leads to other operatives we can discover by following the chain. We cannot afford to be surprised."

"Keep the doors locked and alarms on, and I will see you soon," Richard told Jan as he and Smith left to pack and retrieve the SUV.

"Here is that time pressure you referred to," said Nick.

"Yes, we had a late start, followed by days of decoys and evasion work, and are falling further behind," del Mundo said. "With primary opponents dropping out in waves and free twenty-four-seven media coverage on all outlets, this primary could be a done deal. The constant messaging and dog whistles are creating a mind-numbing normalization of the untrue and the ridiculous. Add in no debates, only pep rallies salted with paid actors as cheerleaders, and the world is witnessing the longest-running fake reality-TV show. The mob mentality has taken hold, and people are literally being brainwashed. We need to ramp up our efforts and must find a means to expose the agenda. With all media occupied by the constant stream of outrageous distractions, we need a different route. Nick, how viable is your link to the rabbi?"

"Still undiscovered, still on good terms, with the questions being locations and scheduling. I think he has been overseas. Not sure of his return."

"OK, we have urgent work to do. Nick, can you research schedules and look for a contact window?" del Mundo asked. "And Kent, can you do some digging into Richard's contacts? It would be good to know that chain so that we are not blindsided."

"No problem. I am on it," they both said.

Richard and Smith were dropped in a light rain at the terminal, Smith wearing Steiger's bright-blue hooded jacket. They went inside to the restroom, where Smith said, "OK, we look clean so far. We'll ride the shuttle to the long-term parking lot. By wearing Steiger's parka, I can put the hood up, crouch a little, and appear to be the same person getting in as the one who got out when you arrived. You just get into the driver's seat and wait without touching the ignition. I will wander a bit while I work my sweeper."

After a slow and uneventful shuttle ride, they walked to the SUV with Smith, from under the parka hood, scanning 360 degrees. Seeing nothing amiss, they continued with Richard settling in behind the wheel. As Smith approached, a low-pitched beep came from the sweeper. Making an adjustment to the device, he came around quietly and got inside.

With another adjustment and a different signal, he said, "You can start it now."

"What was all that?" Richard asked.

"We have a tracking device underneath somewhere, so I had to double-check for any other little toys, which is a negative. Let's get out of the airport and then head east."

As they moved east on the freeway, Smith dug more equipment from his pack and did some wiring. Soon he was studying a device with a screen and a sweeping arc line like a radar unit. After making some adjustments and fine-tuning, he muttered, "Got them." Shifting to his navigation, he told Richard, "In two miles is a service plaza. Slow down to a crawl as you enter, and I will bail out. Then pull up to a pump and begin fueling. When you see me approaching, stop fueling and be ready to move out."

As they pulled into the plaza, Smith hopped out and made his way to a small park-like area with a few hedges and small trees. Slipping unnoticed into the cover, he took a knee and watched his screen. Soon a low hum became more pronounced as a large, nondescript sedan entered the plaza. He snapped pictures and watched as the car pulled up to a pump away from the SUV. As the driver started his pump and headed for the convenience store, Smith strolled by the car, bent down to tie a shoe, and quickly placed a transmitter inside the bumper. About the size of a quarter, with a remote-power on/off function, it would be almost impossible to detect. With another swift move, he punctured a tire with a thin pick and inserted an old screw, creating what would appear to be a random medium-slow leak. Getting into the SUV with Richard, he said only, "We should go now."

Within minutes after entering the service plaza, they were back on the freeway, still headed east. Smith interrupted the transmission from the tracker under them and told Richard, "We can do a U-turn and head back west to take I-5 north."

"Yes, sir." After several minutes, Richard asked, "What happened back there?"

"I was tracking our tracker. He would get gas, maybe try for a visual of us, then go into the store for supplies, a very unremarkable appearing person. Meanwhile, we now have a microtransmitter with him, and maybe there is a small delay in his near future. Now let's put down the hammer because it is a long drive to your place."

As Richard drove, Smith monitored his assortment of gadgets. With the encrypted sat phone, he contacted *Madeline/Veritas*. "Smith here. We are in motion again after losing a small parade from airport parking. We are running clean for now, and I am forwarding you a connection to a tracker traveling with chasers. They appear to have a wheel issue and may be delayed. I'm also sending pictures of unit and driver. Let's see where this one leads."

"Roger. Will source. Good job." said Nick.

With the incoming data, Nick booted up and began with the license plate, which did not get a hit in the public database. The next database identified the plates as registered to a foreign embassy. Nick reported this to del Mundo and said, "Guess which one."

"That figures. Maybe Smith can trap a hiker at Richard's," del Mundo said.

"Meanwhile, I will begin a data search of the two people Richard contacted. Fortunately, he gave them no details of what we are sitting on. Unfortunately, it appears that some clues he mentioned have been forwarded up a command chain. Let's remember that Richard had no connection to the *Veritas,* so any interest in him could come only from someone he contacted. And that conjecture is valid only if the hikers are more than hikers. Simply put, if the hikers are innocents, then these contacts could have no questionable connections. Either way, the data search of these media persons could have ties to the agenda perpetrators, knowingly or unknowingly. In summary, this search could prove meaningless or not."

"Very profound conclusion," del Mundo said. "We both have much searching in our immediate future. Let's get on with it."

"Roger that."

"And Steiger can be pressed into service to lighten this load," del Mundo said.

"Roger that too." Nick was smiling.

While these three began the search, Richard and Smith were in midst of a long road trip. Alternating driving and sleeping, they took only fuel stops and grabbed sandwiches and coffee to go. Keeping pace with traffic in busy areas and ramping up speed as much as road and conditions would permit in sparse rural areas, they were making good time. Within his assortment of electronics, Smith carried sophisticated radar detectors, which made high speeds possible. High speed for Smith did have an elevated level compared with that of Richard.

"Why don't you rest while I'm hauling ass, and then I can nap while you negotiate the slower traffic zones?" Smith said.

"Sounds good. Don't crash; you might wake me up," Richard said.

"I'll try to avoid any inconveniences."

In the hanger, on *Madeline/Veritas*, a break was called for lunch and a rest of the eyes. Over soup, sandwiches, and coffee, they compared notes.

"First, given a tracking transmitter showing up on Richard's SUV, the likelihood of innocent hikers seems slim. Richard has made no mention of any current or recent work on sensitive issues. Since they checked for trackers before they left the house, the device had to have been placed in the airport parking lot. This could have followed a simple scan of West Coast airport parking. They could have begun with SeaTac and then expanded the search southward. The Canadian border surveillance soon would have ruled out that direction. That this contact and follow-up produced a tracker insertion so quickly points to a large-scale operation and is a clue to the depth and seriousness of the plot.

"While Smith's tire trick had not been detected after many uses, a faulty transmitter on their vehicle, while not unusual, could reveal their efforts. A reaction might include increased surveillance of Richard's world, with steps to backtrack his travels. This should prove to be a dead end, but with missing days and hours, cross-checking of surrounding areas and airport cameras could turn up something. Therefore, we need to increase our security procedures here at the nest and do our own monitoring of camera feeds for this time frame." Nick and Steiger chewed on this sobering logic from del Mundo along with sandwiches.

Lunch ended quickly, and they all returned to the task with an ever-increasing sense of urgency. After another hour of working, Steiger spoke up. "Richard contacted a Jeremy Fields, a Fox News analyst. It turns out that Fields is close to an Eastern European oil company CEO from his days reporting from overseas. With this oligarch spending much time in the United States, they have easily remained in contact. This guy is known to have close ties with the Russian gas and oil conglomerate. Do we just love coincidences or what?"

"This entire action is so blatant and the public statements so hypocritical that they are insulting," said Nick. "And Richard stumbled into the worst possible media contact."

"Yes, and after no public reaction or objection to the many blatant lies made by the campaign, we should not be surprised at the ease of manipulating a low-information electorate," del Mundo said.

On that note, they all returned to their screens.

On the interstate, slowing down from well north of one hundred miles per hour, Smith woke up Richard with a rapid deceleration. "Hey, welcome back. You missed lots of nice hills and curves. We are coming to a fuel stop still running clean, and I figured you might want coffee since we need you to drive from here on in."

"Where are we?" Richard asked sleepily.

"About four hours out."

Checking his watch, Richard gasped. "How did that happen?"

"I have this old war wound nerve damage in my right foot, and it must have fallen asleep and kept the gas pedal stuck to the floor."

"Why did I ask?"

"Here is the story," Smith said. "We need to arrive at your place appearing the same as when you left, not that I think you were observed at that time. Rather, consistency is good. Here we are. Let's make this quick. Fill tanks, drain tanks, coffee and munchies to go, and we roll. We want to arrive before first light."

Minutes later, they were cruising north again, with Richard at the wheel.

"I need your help with some intel," Smith said. "First, where exactly is Steiger's car parked? Second, where does Jan park? And third, how close are your nearest neighbors?"

Realizing that Smith's playful mood had passed, Richard told him that Steiger's car was in the closed shed next to the guesthouse, Jan parked in the attached garage at the main house, and two neighbor families were within a quarter mile.

"Are you in the city, county, or what?"

"Outside city limits but in the county."

"OK, all good. When we get close, slow down some so I can work my gear, then pull in and stop normally."

"That would also be in the garage using the automatic opener."

"Excellent," said Smith. "I'm sure it will be good for you to be home, and I'll bet Jan will be happier also."

"That is a winning bet."

The neighborhood was quiet as the SUV climbed the driveway in darkness. After the garage door closed behind them, Jan came out and ran to Richard for a hug.

Turning and seeing Smith, she said, "Hello, you're not Steiger."

"No, ma'am, I'm Smith. We wanted to get your husband home quickly, and Steiger was busy."

"Well, thank you for that," she said. "I am not usually the nervous type, but all this extra activity has gotten me concerned."

"It looks as if one of my media friends is not really friendly," Richard told her.

"Do we know which one of the two this is?" Jan asked.

"Not yet. We have been driving nonstop, but I will contact the team now, and they may have some details," Smith said while dialing.

"When did you last see the hikers, and how many different ones have there been?"

"One man and a man and woman," she said, "but their paths and direction were not really on any regular routes. I have seen them all twice each over the past day and a half. Would you guys like something to eat? It is almost light out, and I could use some breakfast."

"You didn't say your wife was a mind reader," said Smith. "I'll be online for a while working up a bigger appetite. Thanks."

Over ham and eggs, Smith explained what the team had learned about Fields at Fox. They also found a writers conference at Palm Springs that week and added Richard and Steiger to the list of attendees. An article was being published in local newspapers about the conference with a mention of Richard. This should provide some cover and hopefully turn down the heat.

"Del Mundo felt that Steiger's vehicle should remain out of sight in the shed. It appears that surveillance emanating from the Fields contact began with locating the SUV at John Wayne parking. With the conference cover planted, the loop should be closed. Keeping the Steiger vehicle hidden for now is prudent. He suggested that you both stay home for now and, if possible, remain unseen. And take some pictures of your hikers if they reappear if you can do so unobserved. I will take a walk later and meet a driver who will take me to Paine Field for a private flight back south. We will remain in close contact. You can point me to an unused path through the woods to meet my driver, if you don't mind."

With Smith preparing for his walk and the Douglas family ready for in-home time, the pressure was strong on board the *Madeline/ Veritas*.

"We will monitor Richard's home to be certain there is no further activity there. With the primary turning in favor of our boy and other candidates being forced out in groups, unbelievable as it seems, the nomination may be already secured. With the constant media drumming and the weaknesses of all other candidates, the trend is toward this result. Nick, I think you should schedule a meeting in DC or wherever your rabbi is. We are already running behind, and the pace of events is problematic. After losing precious days with our survival evasions, it is crucial that we bring all possible firepower into play. At this point, we can hold back nothing as this crazy plan looks less far-fetched every day," del Mundo said.

"Agreed," said Nick, turning to begin the protocol of contacting the rabbi.

Chapter 6

* * *

TEAM GOES PROACTIVE, MOBILE

Beginning a contact ritual that could involve days, Nick was shocked when, after switching phone and radio, the "rabbi" was live on the sat phone.

"That was quick," boomed the rabbi. "Hey, wait a minute. My messenger won't arrive on your island for at least a half hour. Interesting. How soon can you be in DC?"

"Mom's home. I'm not. I can be there myself by morning, tomorrow evening with Mom," Nick said.

"See you both for dinner then. Use normal protocol." And the line went dead.

Nick signaled del Mundo to lose his headset.

"My rabbi has a messenger arriving at the island as we speak," he said.

"What? I thought you were starting your contact ritual," del Mundo said.

"I did, but he was way ahead of me. He is back in DC and expecting Mom and me tomorrow for dinner."

"Of course, he told you nothing."

"Of course."

The rabbi's brief conversation and abrupt sign-off were nothing new to Nick, nor was this bothersome to him. After many years and several delicate missions, Nick instantly switched to a different mind-set after hearing the request to bring Mom.

"Mom" was a 110-pound female Rottweiler who had been Nick's working partner through several harrowing situations, in combat and undercover modes. Trained in verbal and nonverbal commands with multiple skills in detection, tracking, and various levels of security, Mom was alert and formidable at work but a gentle and friendly pet at home. Growing up with Nick twenty-four-seven from six weeks old, she was totally devoted to her master and so attuned that at times she seemed to read his mind. Now four, spayed, and athletic, Mom was the best working partner Nick had known.

Troubling, though, was Mom's requested presence. Even knowing how much the rabbi welcomed her company and how much his children enjoyed playing with her, Nick realized that this request meant something more serious than happy kids, big and little, playing with Mom.

Nick and Mom going to work involved a certain amount of preparation. There was a collapsible lightweight alloy kennel with a soft blanket. There was a harness rack for large cargo and a backpack type of service vest with the logo "Service Animal Do Not Touch" on both sides. Nick joked that Mom acted like she loved her vest so he would think she loved work, but he knew it was all about the Milk-Bones or other groceries riding there. Mom was an easy companion for Nick. She usually spoke only when asked or as an alert and was generally friendly.

For Nick, work meant an outdated worn suit, a top-coat, a hat, and thick rubber-soled brogans. With gray hair dye, a cane, a slight stoop, and a limp, he appeared to be nonthreatening and unmemorable. For a decorated special forces veteran, world-class athlete, and martial arts and weapons master, the rumpled persona he projected was Oscar quality. More than once, this disguise had proved its value. Being underestimated led to his survival. He would pack two sets of work clothes, some black cargo pants, turtlenecks, jackets, and boots, a knitted watch hat, toiletries kit, four sets of underwear and socks, and assorted electronics and hardware. For day or night action, with new age organic spray hair dyes, Mom could be a blonde by day and a natural brunette by night.

On his island, in addition to his home, Nick also had a comfortable caretaker cottage, home of Otto, a six-foot-seven-inch retired British special forces and intelligence veteran in his early sixties. With Otto lived his wife, Helga, a Swedish beauty of about the same age, who was an artist, gourmet chef, and more. Both were unwaveringly loyal to Nick and Mom, who in true Rottweiler form looked after them both and sought to keep them organized.

"How about a military executive shuttle from Pendleton to Whidbey Island and then a chopper to your place? Chopper pickup in the morning back to Whidbey and then a charter jet for you and Mom to DC?" del Mundo asked.

"Sounds good. Can you keep Steiger here with you to help with the large amount of research requests that are sure to be heading your way?" Nick asked.

"Great idea. I'm sure we will both be needed. And, Nick, will you pass this to your rabbi?" Del Mundo handed him a thick envelope.

"Sure."

Having come to the barn directly from his "get lost" tour, Nick had minimal packing and was soon being driven by Smith to Pendleton for his ride north. The plane was already fueled, checked, and ready and went wheels up immediately after he boarded. The only other passenger already on board was a four-star marine general he didn't know. After a shake of hands and exchanges of good mornings, they were both napping as they gained altitude to cruising level. Nick was happy remaining anonymous and catching up on needed sleep. Upon landing and waking up, Nick said, "Nice talking with you, sir."

The general laughed and said, "Nice talking with you too, sir."

After transferring to a Jet Ranger and a short, low-altitude ride to his island, he was home. The chopper barely touched down so he could disembark and then was gone, thumping back to Whidbey.

Nick had barely put his feet on the ground when Mom raced to him, rubbing against his legs and snuffling, all wriggles and glee.

"Hey, Mom, how's my partner?" Nick asked as he scratched her ears and back. Mom whined happily, and life was good for them both.

"That is some quick action. The messenger just dropped off a note for you," Otto announced as he shook Nick's hand.

"I had a phone call advising of the letter and content," Nick said. "Mom and I are being picked up in the morning by the same taxi that just dropped me here. Let's have a bite of dinner, if we can find something, and I can fill you in on what is going on."

"Helga, being a part-time psychic and part-time gourmet chef, has been in your kitchen for hours creating the daily special," Otto said with a smile.

"You are wise to not attempt any interference in your wife's projects," Nick said.

"More hungry than wise, I'm afraid," Otto replied.

They made their way to the house, with a happy Mom wriggling and hopping along with them.

"There you are, just in time for chicken piccata with fixings and a pretty fair French rosé," Helga said as she reached for her hug.

"I won't ask how you knew I would be here for dinner."

"I could say that a little bird told me or say that Otto and I were planning on having a feast for ourselves, so believe what you must."

Nick was chuckling with Helga until he noticed that the table had been set for three and that the amounts of the various courses were obviously much greater than a dinner for two.

"I'm not real sure about you sometimes, Helga," Nick said.

"Neither is Otto, and I consider these facts to be a worthy achievement on my part."

Nick smiled and said, "Otto, you were correct when you advised me not to start up with Helga."

They all laughed as they sat, with Mom taking her usual position lying near the door.

They ate silently for a while and savored the delicious meal. "Helga, how can you possibly continue to outdo yourself?" Nick asked when he stopped chewing for a minute.

"Nick, why don't you stop with the flattery and tell us what is going on?" she replied.

"Nothing too exciting," Nick said. "Just an invitation from my old friend to bring Mom for a visit to DC. We're being picked up in the morning and will be out of your way again."

"You are hopeless. You know that you are never in my way, and I doubt that Mom was asked to join you so she could play with your friend's kids."

"You are, as usual, very perceptive, but please don't tell Mom and spoil her trip before she leaves."

"Yes, like she won't know you are packing for work, which you know is something she loves, even though you find some juvenile humor with pretending to question her work ethic."

"Aw, she knows I am not serious with all that."

They went back to eating and drinking as Mom groaned and stretched, happy as always to be the subject of conversation.

Morning came early, and Nick dressed in his work clothes: the old suit, the topcoat, and the rest. Most packing had been finished after dinner, so only a few items needed to be added, among them a seldom-used but handy Glock nine millimeter and his assortment of knives, which he always carried. With her regular load of kennels, leashes, and vests, Mom would carry her own supplies as always, including the bag of concentrated high-protein kibble and a supply of Milk-Bones. After a light breakfast, the thump of rotors signaled their departure time. With Mom a white dog this morning, they loaded the gear, boarded the same Jet Ranger, and were off. Landing at the base, they moved quickly from the chopper into a nearby Cessna Citation II and settled in for a cross-country luncheon cruise.

After a rest and a box lunch for Nick and some kibble and a Milk-Bone for Mom, Nick said, "We still don't know what the rabbi's urgent call is all about."

"Aargh," groaned Mom.

"You always say that," Nick told her.

"Woof," she responded.

"Hopeless beast," he chided, which was followed by her long whine.

Staying far above the storms blanketing the Midwest, the flight was a smooth one, as was the landing.

"Hey, this doesn't look like Dulles," Nick told the pilot.

"Good eye, sir. We changed the flight plan to land at this private field in Virginia. We will taxi directly to the van you see by the service area."

This on-the-fly change in flight plan was another clue to the trip's gravity, or at least to the rabbi's level of concern.

After loading their gear, they were soon in the van on the freeway and stopped at a Holiday Inn just outside Washington. They checked in, dropped off most of their gear, and were headed to dinner, Nick in his work clothes and Mom in the service vest, which she knew carried the Milk-Bones among other necessities. They were dropped off in an alley at the service entrance of a small boutique hotel in Georgetown. They were greeted by a nondescript man wearing a suit and an earbud. Making their way through empty corridors and upstairs to a mezzanine level, they were shown to a private dining room with two more security types at the door. The rabbi met them as the door closed.

"Mom, great to see you. Thanks for bringing your employee." Mom wriggled up for an ear scratch with a little whine.

"Thanks for the promotion. The last time you used that line, I was the temp," Nick said as they shook hands.

"She gave you a good evaluation for the last quarter. Now please sit."

"Thank you," said Nick, taking a seat at the table while Mom followed command and sat at attention by the door.

"Can you tell Mom to relax?" the rabbi asked.

"Sure. Mom, I know you were told to sit, but you can chill now." Mom stretched out and groaned contentedly.

"I forgot how literal your boss is."

"Happens to me frequently."

"First question, Nick, is how you happened to be contacting me before my summons reached you."

"I have been involved with del Mundo after passing a package for him and taking a round-the-globe 'get lost' jaunt. This package is toxic, and he had spent days eluding determined pursuers. He realized that this package outlined a serious national threat that was moving at a faster pace than he could overtake. He felt that you might be the only one with the power who could thwart this attack. I agreed with his conclusion and request and began our contact protocol. And there you were, same day, same time, and speaking live. I have been wondering why you needed to see me while I was in the process of reaching out to you."

"Why don't you tell me about this package?" the rabbi said.

Nick told him about del Mundo's stormy arrival by sea with the story of the package ending up in his hands. After relating the story of sending the package to the writer, going on his trip, and del Mundo's oceanic adventures, he handed over the copy of the package, along with the envelope that del Mundo asked Nick to pass to his rabbi. As the rabbi scanned the material, his expression changed from a scowl to great surprise.

"This is uncanny," he said. "We have been watching this show for some time, and this document just confirms our fears and more. Our analysts and psychologists have consistently speculated about collusion between the candidate and Russian influence. We were already confident of our conclusions, and this package confirms them. I was summoning you for a mission, which ironically deals with the same situation that del Mundo wanted you to enlist my help with. Now that is a strange circle. The narrative is complex, and we must be careful as our democracy is under serious attack, a cyber-manipulative attack that is progressing rapidly. The mission I have in mind is extremely delicate, and we believe your involvement is our best course of action, though the outcome could be unpredictable. Let's have our dinner before it is cold, and then I will explain."

The dinner was excellent, though their enjoyment was limited by the circumstances they were discussing. Mom was restless, responding to the tones of the conversation.

After the meal, the rabbi said, "We began with reports of questionable loans, banking, and luxury real estate purchases by certain Russian oligarchs. Some of these transactions included involvement with the candidate's various business entities. These connections were repeatedly surfacing in different countries, including our own. Red flags continued to come up, and deeper investigation revealed violations of international and US law, which presented us with a difficult choice. Do we pursue litigation, which, though successful, could easily be misconstrued and labeled a 'political witch-hunt'? This course of action might be effective regarding US citizens but would allow the foreign actors to scatter and avoid our reach. We decided to continue our evidence gathering, build a case, and let this candidacy play itself out. At that point, we could apprehend all suspects and allow justice to be served.

"We were all surprised at the embrace of a divisive, fear-based message by a large segment of the electorate. We now know that the Republican nomination is already a done deal, to the surprise of many. We, of the off-the-books committee of which you are familiar, had another meeting to update and revisit our strategy. We decided to continue our investigation and monitoring but also to consider a backup plan to deal with unforeseen election results. As the Russian interference with cyber attacks and misinformation increased and the electorate growing more polarized, we wanted an ace in the hole.

"The committee was unanimous in requesting you to be our ace, as you have been previously with much success. We must remember that there are two separate issues in play here, both significant threats to our democracy. One issue is the Russian interference in our presidential election, with the goal of harming one candidate while helping the other. The other issue is a massive money-laundering scheme by Russian oligarchs of hundreds of billions of dollars stolen from nationalized corporate entities. Several of these efforts included the cooperation of one or more international banks, some that have since been discovered and paid large penalties. Other foreign banks that have been and are still involved have known criminals as directors as well as members of the candidate's team.

"The candidate has many business involvements with huge real estate transactions that appear to be part of the money-laundering scheme of these oligarchs. Here is the rub, Nick. The candidate, while certainly an obvious, juicy target, must not be our target, which would have us falling into a trap. He is only the TV show, the distraction. All his statements and actions, regardless of their ridiculousness, are designed for the sole purpose of dominating and driving the news cycle. Unfortunately, we now have a bumper sticker fake reality-show mentality in our country, and these tactics are well planned and have been very effective. For us to focus on and target the candidate would be a mistake, the trap. At any point, the controllers could deem him expendable and stage some drama show that removes him, and we would be left holding air with another of their compromised figureheads taking over. At this point, our ability to prosecute the major culprits in both scams would be greatly diminished.

"We have for many months been funneling donations to this candidate's campaign through a political action committee that has so far remained anonymous, with no stated representatives or contributors. We would like for you to assume the role of representative of this group, with the actual donors remaining anonymous. In this position, you will be viewed by the campaign as a cash supporter and as such will be welcomed and afforded an amount of access and inclusion. With this posture, you will be able to monitor events and conversations and pass information to us while portraying a quiet, reclusive ally. Again, while the outside influence in our election process is a problem, we must not chase the diversion but instead concentrate on the Russian actors as the primary targets. While yours is mostly a passive role, the ever-changing situation could conceivably require you to take extreme action, which could include protecting the candidate from his Russian handlers should he become expendable to them. Should he be unreasonable when confronted with his options, your job might entail his apprehension and spiriting away from his keepers. Any options you may face will have serious consequences and must be undertaken with the greatest of care and security. We need you in place to counter any unexpected events. These are the conditions that have led to our call to you and Mom."

This was a quite a large download, a complicated story, which Nick needed time to process and analyze. "That is a lot to consider," he said.

"You are correct. That is a lot to consider, and that is just a quick peek. Let's take a short break, have dessert and coffee, and then chat some more."

"Sounds good to me. How about you, Mom?"

"Rrrff."

Apple pie finished and coffee served, the rabbi continued. "I realize this plan may sound like cloak-and-dagger, but remember that the committee is off the books with a security clearance several levels beyond classified. Your own experience with the committee tells you that we are neither frivolous nor political, serving only as a last-ditch protector of our democracy."

"I can see the value and need for a presence in proximity to this campaign, but I'm wondering what an emergency option might entail."

"We knew you would have that question. Our thinking is that at some point, we might decide to confront the candidate with the evidence already in hand and attempt to convert him to a double agent and join our efforts to save the nation. If this effort is unsuccessful, even after the outlining of existing evidence and what his exposure would be, including asset seizure and prosecution, certainly impeachment, then we would be compelled to consider options. We could create a narrative of his patriotic cooperation, which might appear beneficial to him. This would be true on one level but would probably lead to his becoming expendable to the Russians. Other options could cause the same result but with seemingly different methods. In summary, you might need to handle his conversion and subsequent protection, or the opposite."

"Any attempt to turn him would immediately blow my cover and, depending on the location of the discussion, could be immediately hazardous to my health," Nick said.

"That is true, so for this option to be viable, your 'donor' acceptance will need to allow you to select the location for this talk. And, of course Mom will have your back."

"Woof," from Mom, hearing her name.

"As I suspected, the usual story. It will all be on me, with deniability from all quarters. I should be accustomed to these conditions by now, but I would need one small concession," Nick said. "If turning him is unsuccessful and I find myself in imminent danger, I need the ability to use any other survival option for me and/or our democracy that is available."

"I will inform the committee that you are willing to take the mission, subject to your blanket approval to undertake any actions that you deem vital for survival of both you and the democracy."

"And for Mom's survival also."

"Of course, done."

"When do we start?" Nick asked.

"We already have. I have a rather thick packet of info for you. You will have a day or two to absorb this data, get used to your new identity, and prepare to relocate closer to the action. Thank you for your service, as always, and have a good night's rest." With that, the rabbi headed for the door and his security detail, giving Mom an ear scratch on his way.

Chapter 7

●　●　●

MAN AND DOG GO TO WORK

Following an uneventful van ride back to the Holiday Inn, Nick and Mom slipped out a garage entrance for a needed stroll. After a slow perimeter lap around the immediate area, checking for any watchers or abnormalities, with no alerts, they found a secluded wooded area nearby. Here they could have an exercise session and a jog, away from uninvited eyes. With Nick in his night gear and Mom having been showered back to her natural black, on this moonless night they were practically invisible. They worked out and ran in silence, using hand signals and body language to communicate directions, speed, and postures. After more than an hour of nonstop practice and running, in a lather, they went back to the garage, climbed the stairs, and returned to their room unseen by people or cameras. After a quick shower, they were both ready for rest.

"Well, Mom, that was needed and fun."

"Woof."

"Did you want a nighty-night Milk-Bone?"

"Arrwoof."

"I knew that. You're a good girl."

Mom was chewing noisily as Nick dropped into a deep sleep.

The next morning, room service left a tray of omelet, bacon, home fries, toast, and coffee, along with a copy of the *Washington Post*. While Nick had a leisurely breakfast, he skimmed through the paper and then started on the thick file from the rabbi.

"Good morning to you too," he said to a kibble-crunching partner.

"Rr-r," Mom sounded between bites.

The file traced the candidate's contacts and dealings with Russia over the past twenty years, back to a beauty pageant staged in Moscow. This event brought him into contact with Vladimir Putin, which allowed the dictator his initial observations of the candidate's strengths and weaknesses. Putin liked what he saw: an accomplished flimflam man who had managed to gain access to large amounts of capital and properties. The history of his many large ventures, included bankruptcies resulting with partners absorbing huge losses while he profited, were intriguing to the Russian. The combination of a conscienceless robbing of business partners and then the manipulation of US bankruptcy laws to his benefit could signal interesting possibilities. Further consideration of uncontrollable sexual proclivities added considerably to vulnerability and possible usefulness long term. Some reports detailing staged and filmed encounters with prostitutes while in Russia could prove persuasive at some time and were added to the dossier.

There were hints of Russian steering of the candidate's TV career as a character of unquestionable authority, the ultimate boss whose pronouncements were beyond any challenge. Though viewed solely as entertainment at the time, this multiyear fake reality-TV effort also served the purpose of subliminally training the large US audience that the face they were watching was the face of the final word, the boss of all. At this point in the narrative, Nick began to feel nauseated by the depth and long-term complexity of the groundwork as described. The fact that this process remained unnoticed for so long was almost disorienting. Mom, feeling his unease, gave a low whine.

"You are right, girl. We seem to be in a dicey situation."

"Rrwoof."

"How can you agree when you haven't even read the report?"

"Arrrr."

"Thanks for trusting me."

Mom wriggled and stretched.

Nick decided that they could both use a walk. "Let's break out your partial-disguise gear and head to the woods."

"Woof rrrr."

Nick helped Mom into the brilliant white sweater with half legs and service vest, along with a serious-looking muzzle, which was constructed of easy tear-away fabric. This piece was easy for Mom to tolerate, being only a featherweight, easily losable source of an extra Milk-Bone. With Nick in the old-guy suit and cane, now also with dark glasses, they were out the service entrance and headed for the perimeter route. With the neighborhood appearing normal, they slowly made their way to the woods, where Mom could perform her daily rituals. While trained to use bathtubs or showers for urination, she usually waited for a no-maintenance area for her stool. After less than a day, she already loved this area. Out of sight, they had a brief exercise session. They emerged taking up the slow, stooped gait of the old disabled fellow with his dog at his side. Back to the service entrance and up to the room, Nick was going for the shower when he heard the whine.

"Sorry, you're right—you earned a Milk-Bone, so let me have the muzzle before you ruin it." Mom crunched happily as Nick took his shower.

With a fresh cup of coffee and his partner snoozing by the door, Nick was soon deep into the intel report, which now detailed some of the candidate's business dealings. Included were many foreign joint ventures, partnerships, licensing agreements, corporations—hundreds of ventures and entities. Upon closer examination, the numbers involved in many of these transactions, on the surface, made no sense. Why would investors pay large sums more than appraised value for properties or many times competitive bids for development projects? Further research of several such cases revealed a common theme, found in different nations. The common denominator within these illogical deals was financing with large cash amounts from Russians or Russian surrogates. Illogical became logical when the real goal was the laundering of cash plundered from nationalized industries by despotic rulers, international drug cartels, or families fronting for organized terrorist groups. Deutsche Bank was nearly drowned in a scandal involving Russian actors, was fined millions of dollars, and was forced to terminate top managers. One or more of these executives moved to the Bank of Cyprus, where an American investor soon made a large investment and became the largest stockholder and managing partner. Some of these business arrangements had direct or indirect ties to the candidate. Other data mentioned probable Russian hackers providing WikiLeaks with e-mails damaging to the Democratic candidate. Raising more questions was the candidate's continual praise of the Russian president, even comparing his performance favorably with that of the democratically elected president of the United States, and the candidate's statements of how much he loved WikiLeaks, going so far as to suggest that the organization should find more e-mails to further damage his opponent. Having absorbed a large amount of this troubling information, Nick was ready for a break.

As if on schedule, his phone rang, and following the usual clicks and beeps was the rabbi's altered voice. "Your van will arrive in two hours for transport to your new digs. I trust the accommodations will be adequate, and please give your boss an ear scratch for me." Click.

"That was your friend, ordering me to scratch your ears."

"Rrrrrr," Mom sounded as he scratched.

Back to the report, Nick skipped down to details of his new assumed identity and legend. He was aware of John Hawkins, but it had been years since his creation, so he needed to refresh his memory. He would be a disabled retired economics professor from a small Midwestern college with partial blindness and serious injuries sustained in a car crash. After surgeries and laser for his eyes, he was ambulatory and used a service dog. "Hey, Mom, good news: you are included in my new identity."

"Woof."

The report also included details of the fictional political action committee Patriots for Strong Leaders, for which he would be the representative. This PAC had been registered two years previously and was a donor from the beginning of the campaign, though a note explained that it was not expected to ever be put into play. This history highlighted the committee's vision and attention to detail, and Nick was impressed but not surprised. "It appears that the rabbi has been diligent as usual."

"Ruff."

"Uneducated redundancy."

"Arrrr."

Reading further, Nick learned that they would be staying in a small brownstone a few blocks from the tower campaign headquarters. Seeing the address, he remembered the acquisition years ago by the committee. He was happy to learn that while being well maintained and staffed by a maid/cook and a sometime handyman and butler, it had never before been used in an operation. The accommodations could be a lot worse, as in most of his other assignments, but Nick was too experienced for expectations and knew firsthand how quickly a beautiful day could morph into a metaphorical tsunami. Checking his watch, Nick began sorting and packing. Feigning sleep, Mom was up the second he touched his duffel, heading for her gear, walking almost sideways with all the wriggling, grinning happily.

"You are quite the actress, sleepyhead. A real piece of work."

"Woof."

They were quickly packed and on I-95 north to arrive after dark, Nick in his work garb, Mom in the white sweater and service vest, no muzzle. Their ride was another generic white van, though the mirrored windows were bullet-proof, and the interior had been designed in the luxury-jet style with captain chairs and a couch—all in butter-soft leather—a TV, a sink, a small bath, a fridge, a microwave, satellite phone and Wi-Fi. Against normal furniture rules, Nick signaled Mom to a captain chair.

"Rrrrrr?" from a hesitant Mom.

"I know, but we are technically working, so I will make an exception in the goal of enhanced mission visual range," he told her.

"Arrwoof." Resigned, Mom hopped up and got comfortable, with her chin resting on the windowsill.

"And try not to drool on the upholstery."

This was ignored.

Traffic was average, and as they reached their destination the street was quiet, with a light drizzle making everything shiny. In the alley was a walled rear entrance and a wide door, possibly a garage. Nick, seeing nothing suspicious as the van moved slowly down the alley, lowered a window to sniff the air, which Mom was already doing. When they stopped beside the door, Nick opened the slider and signaled "sweep" to Mom and got out of the way. In a matter of seconds, she had checked the entire alley, the buildings, doors, and Dumpsters, and was back smiling and sitting in the "OK" position. As they unloaded the gear, the door swung open soundlessly.

"Welcome, Mr. Hawkins and Ms. Mom. Please come in." The soft voice belonged to a big-boned, blond-haired woman possibly in her fifties. "I was told to keep an eye out and to see that you are comfortable."

"Thank you, but I am at a disadvantage. You know who I am, but I don't believe I have had the pleasure," Nick said.

Blushing slightly, she said, "I am so sorry. I am Helen Swenson."

Taking her hand, Nick told her, "It is good to meet you, Helen, and I would like you to meet my partner, Mom."

Mom, who had already checked out Helen, was pleased and moved in for a nuzzle and an ear scratch.

"Oh, what a sweetheart you are," Helen told her and scratched as expected.

"Mom, you are so bad," Nick told her. "Helen went for the sheepish look, and you are getting the full treatment." To Helen, he said, "It is only fair to tell you that Mom does like you."

"Aargh."

"It is nice to all be on the same page. I don't think you are so bad, Mom," Helen said.

"Woof."

"I need help," Nick muttered.

"If you would like to get settled into your upstairs quarters, I'll see if I can find something for dinner."

"Yes, ma'am." They carried the gear up, Mom in the lead.

On the second-floor landing, Nick removed Mom's cargo rack, opened doors, and gave the sweep sign. She was soon back with the smile, and Nick pointed down the stairs and signaled, and she was bounding back down. While Nick moved their gear into a spacious master suite, he smelled savory cooking aromas wafting up the stairs, followed by Mom. When she was sitting at OK after her sweep, Nick told her what a good girl she was and handed her a Milk-Bone. His hunger was great, and the kitchen smells were too good, so he left the unpacking and headed downstairs. With the brief Milk-Bone moment over, Mom scrambled up and hit the bottom of the stairs beside her partner.

"What do I smell?" Nick asked as they entered the kitchen.

"I found some lobster bisque and a bucket of oysters, which are almost ready to come out of the frying pan."

As Nick examined the bisque, he asked with a raised eyebrow, "You just found this?"

"Well, I found pieces here and there."

"And you had no idea whether I liked pan-fried oysters, right?"

"You can't believe everything you hear."

"Mom, your good judgment is still intact."

"Woofrr."

Helen just chortled and began plating the meal. "And what for your boss?" she asked with a smile.

"I see the vicious rumors have preceded me. She could probably have a little lobster juice on her kibble. Better let me do it, or she won't touch it."

"I know who the boss is."

"I can see that we will have such a fun time here."

"I doubt that a large amount of fun time is in your near future, but I would bet that Mom has fun even when she is not having fun."

"You have been well briefed."

"Woof."

Dinner was pleasant and delicious.

Over the years, Nick had heard of the legendary Swede, Helen, who was the subject of much agency lore within a certain building. Her risky missions had always been successful, and she maintained a sarcastic good humor even in the tensest of moments. Competent and lethal, she had a casual manner and accomplishments that earned widespread loyalty. To know Helen was to know a friend. Nick was glad that they could meet and glad for her to be holding down the fort, realizing that for his rabbi to assign this level of base team underscored the importance and inherent danger of his purpose.

It was still early after dinner, so Nick and Mom headed out the alley for a recon walk, moving slowly, staying in character. They stayed on the sidewalk and stopped frequently to look in store windows and at reflections, passing all types of vendors, bars, restaurants, galleries, hotels, and office high-rises. People were out even in the light rain, but none seemed to take much interest in an old limping guy with a service dog. Mom's nose was working at near-maximum capacity with so many smells at once, so she did not mind a slow pace. Eventually, they made their way past the campaign tower and circled the block. The building security was disruptive and oppressive. A parking lane was blocked off and held a fleet of law-enforcement vehicles. There were NYPD, FBI, Secret Service, US Park

Police, and certainly other nonuniformed agency personnel. The street was jammed, and even pedestrian traffic was impeded. It was a madhouse even across the avenue where the man and dog paused as if for breath and then continued with a slow, careful walk.

"It looks like a film shoot around here."

"Woof rrrr."

"You are right. It is the world's longest-running twenty-four-seven fake reality-TV show."

"Woof woof."

As they ambled along the busy streets, counting security personnel, Nick realized that any operations in or around the fortress of the campaign headquarters would need to be accomplished with creative finesse rather than force. As always, Nick found that any time spent with Mom made for a good day, even if only a slow walk or doing nothing, so they were both happy on the damp evening. Ahead, Nick saw a small crowd milling around on the sidewalk, a boom box going hard. As they approached, feeling Mom's light pressure on his leg, he reacted instantly and stepped from the sidewalk to the vacant fire lane. With Mom close, they easily walked past the crowd, which had become a pile after a tipsy couple had tripped and fallen, causing a wave.

"Good steer, Mom."

"Wowoof."

"OK, we have seen enough. Let's head for a little kibble."

Turning onto a quieter street, Mom pressed the pace as much as she thought would be unnoticeable.

"That is OK, but don't push it," Nick said.

Connected and synced like a jockey and horse, Nick and Mom had played catch, dodge, and chase games all her life and enjoyed head games within their never-breached security protocols.

Maintaining the proper pace, they were soon home. Once inside with door and locks secured, Mom stopped, looked at Nick, and cocked her head. Now hit with a strong mint smell, Nick told her, "Don't even ask. Why don't you have a sweep and check on Helen?"

A happy little snort, and she was off. Nick heard "There you are" and the other cooing sounds, then nothing except the soft jazz that had been playing when they arrived. Then the happy woof, and he had to fork over a Milk-Bone. Gladly.

After another night of uninterrupted sleep and Helen's fortifying breakfast of grapefruit, banana, oatmeal, toast, and a protein shake, they were out for the morning walk.

"Let's get coffee at the hornet's nest tower and do a little sniffing around."

"Woof."

After a little park time for Mom's morning business and a leisurely walk to the tower, they made their way, with a few glances but no issues, to the Starbucks on the mezzanine level. With a cup of Kenyan and a newspaper, Nick took a table near the door with enough leg room for Mom to get comfortable out of the flow, out of sight. Watching the morning parade, Nick noticed a young guy in a rumpled suit waiting for a large order of coffees and croissants standing next to the table.

"That sounded like a big order. You must be feeding an army," Nick joked.

"That's pretty close. The campaign staff needs the wake-up cup."

"Very important duty," Nick said.

"Only important until they are served." The man smiled.

"Well said. I wish for you no spills."

"Thanks, have a good one." He left carrying a stack of boxes and never noticed Mom, who was all ears.

"At least the errand boys seem clear eyed," Nick said softly.

"Woof," Mom replied quietly.

As he sipped his coffee, Nick heard snippets of conversation in the busy room. Several languages were spoken, with a surprising amount of Russian. Taking a loose head count, he calculated nearly half the room to be made up of Russians. As they left, the blond Mom in her service vest and faux muzzle steered them, mostly unnoticed, quietly down and out to the street. Outside, the security level was again substantial, possibly even elevated from the night before.

"I think there must be a lot of things going on upstairs."

"Rrwoof."

Taking their time on a roundabout route, Nick, on a double-back, recognized a man from the Starbucks who appeared to be following them but went into a cigar shop as they crossed the street. Taking a position inside an office-building lobby, Nick spent some time examining the directory until seeing the man emerge with a small package and walk back toward the tower.

"Let's go, Mom. We spotted a smoker, not a stalker."

"Woof."

Entering the back door as usual, they smelled this morning's aroma: cinnamon. Mom had a little sneeze before she did her sweep. Again, the "There you are" and the cooing, then the happy grin as the sweep was complete with Mom doing the OK sit, looking at Nick expectantly.

"Yes, good sweep, and you are a good girl," and the Milk-Bone.

Helen came from the kitchen with an envelope for Nick. "The messenger dropped this off about a half hour ago. I hope you have not been out fiddling around with Rome burning."

"For your information, we have only just completed an important recon action and have noticed no unusual smoke, so we could possibly make it through another day."

"Well, aren't you the regular Sherlock Holmes?" Helen smirked on her way back to the kitchen.

Nick had to chuckle as he opened the envelope, which contained a short notice of a meeting for the PAC representative with a Gene Williams of the campaign staff for 1:30 p.m. the next day in one of the lobby bar's private rooms. "Looks like events are moving quickly, Mom, and we have only the rest of the day and the morning to study all the rabbi's intel and perfect our story. We will work in a little stealth excursion this evening, if that is OK with you."

"Wowoof."

After hours of reading and contemplating the report, Nick determined it was clear that the candidate's words and actions were carefully following the agenda from the intercepted package. The TV-show script was well planned and well disciplined, with all players, whether elected officials or hired help, being made to toe the line.

On their nightly walk, this night with Nick in his black cargos, jacket, and cap, Mom in her natural black and without the muzzle, the pace was fast and the route all alleys and shadows. With a quick long-range scan of the tower, still alive with much activity and security, they headed to the park. After a set of exercises and sprints hidden in the trees, they were taking a cool-down walk around the end of the pond. When Nick heard some rustling in the bushes they had just passed, Mom, off leash, moved silently away. Just as Nick heard steps and breathing, there was a loud thump followed by a splash and a curse. Mom rejoined him, and they were gone—a would-be mugger still thrashing and cursing in the water.

"Good bump."

"Rroof."

Home, sleep, and then the day of the first move of the game.

Chapter 8

● ● ●

INTO THE LION'S CAGE, OUT WITH CAPTURED PLAYERS

The sky was clearing, and the partly sunny forecast sounded almost as good as the French toast, maple syrup, yogurt, and fruit of Helen's breakfast offering. Mom was enjoying an ear and back scratch from the chef, her new friend. Well rested and fed, Nick and Mom were ready for the morning walk / exercise routine when Nick's phone buzzed. After some beeps and clicks, his rabbi was speaking.

"The campaign worker you are meeting today, Gene Williams, should prove easy to deal with. He was a staff writer for a right-wing think tank, then campaign manager for one of the early dropout candidates. This campaign hired him after he published over-the-top flattering articles about this candidate. By following our general script, you should have him readily passing you up the chain of command. Remember, our cash donations are the calling card that speaks loudly. Your comments need to emphasize this commitment, offering minimal policy thoughts while making no demands of specific considerations for the PAC. You represent a wealthy group of traditional Midwestern Republicans, older white farmers, proud of their religion-based principles. Being vague about the PAC members' identities will not be challenged by a campaign that eschews science, details, and facts. The overall strategy here is to raise no questions, merely making it easy for Williams to pass you up the line. We are concerned with the many contacts of campaign officials with Russian entities, including business dealings, hackers, and known Russian intelligence agency operatives. The question of collusion or coordination between the campaign and the Russians is valid, so I know you will take note of all campaign staff and Russian individuals you encounter and any attitudes or disagreements you may observe. Good luck, scratch Mom, and we'll have a debriefing afterward." And he was gone.

"Mom, are you still ready to go?"

"Woof."

After a good, uneventful walk and exercise session, they were back home.

"There was a delivery while you were out," said Helen, handing Nick a large envelope.

"Thanks." He headed upstairs to read. After opening the envelope, as Mom was savoring a Milk-Bone, he found a stack of photos with notes. These were Russian operatives and brief backgrounds of each. In the group, he recognized two men who had been in the Starbucks crowd the previous morning. The notes about these two were like a warning. They were suspected of taking extreme actions against dissenters, which included beatings, torture, and disappearances. These were not average campaign workers and could be part of the candidate's claim of having his own security force.

"I was just about to call you," he told Mom as she came upstairs.

"Wowoof."

Now in full character, they walked slowly to the tower, taking rest stops, and were soon in the busy lobby bar. Nick rapped on the door of the private room. After a few seconds, a plain-looking middle-aged man in a coat and tie opened the door, offered his hand, and asked, "Mr. Hawkins?"

Nick shook his hand. "Yes, and you are?"

"Gene Williams. Nice to meet you. Please come in." He took a half step back as he noticed Mom.

"My dog is old like me and equally harmless," Nick said.

"No problem; it seems very calm."

"More like sleepy," Nick assured him.

"May I get you a drink, coffee, snack?"

"Just coffee, thanks. I can fix it myself."

While they sipped their coffees, Williams began. "First, let me thank you and your PAC for your generous support of the campaign. We welcome all who share our vision and wish to join us in making this country

great again. I must admit to not being familiar with
your group, so maybe you could tell me a little about it."

"Yes, of course," Nick said. "We are a small group of
farming families, most tracing their farms back more
than a century This generation has formed a loosely
organized PAC, Patriots for Strong Leaders, to give voice
to our concerns. We are appalled and alarmed at the millions of illegals sneaking across the border from Mexico,
bringing God only knows what drugs, and taking jobs
from American citizens. We want our president to build
a wall, rebuild our military, and stop using our money to
protect every other country in the world. These countries
need us more than we need them. We need more guns
and less Muslims. We could have used this candidate
eight years ago, and by God, we need him now."

Williams, obviously impressed, smiled and said, "We
are indeed grateful for your support and could use more
clear-thinking patriots like you."

"We are just one little group who believe we are under
attack and must fight to protect our way of life," Nick said
earnestly.

"It is certainly a pleasure to meet you, Mr. Hawkins.
Are you in town for a while?"

"A relative of one of our members inherited a little-
used place here that he offered for my stay. My main purpose for the visit is to touch base with the campaign, see
how things are going, and learn what more we can do, if
anything, to help."

The "what more we can do" hinted at more donations. Williams said, "You know, we have a cocktail hour for our staff tomorrow in the bigger private room, and maybe you would like to join us and meet some team members."

"That sounds like a good idea. What time?"

"Six thirty to nine, or thereabouts. You can come early and stay late. Or come late and leave early."

Nick chuckled, country boy that he now was. "Thanks for the invite, Mr. Williams. See you tomorrow."

"Good, but it's Gene."

"Gene it is, then."

They shook hands again, and Nick and Mom walked slowly through the lobby to the exit. As they did the usual slow gait with rest stops, Nick noticed a tall man in a hat and topcoat seeming to match their pace from a half block behind. While they took a meandering course, stopping to look in store windows and at a newsstand for the *Journal,* the follower kept the same distance.

"Time for a little fun," Nick told Mom.

"Arrff."

Slowly turning a corner, coming to a hotel entrance with a cab stand, they got into the only waiting cab, gave directions away from the follower, and sped off. In the side mirror, Nick saw the man come to the hotel, turn a circle, and wave his arm for a cab, to no avail. Turning at the next intersection, Nick and Mom were gone, with no indication that they were aware of being tailed. After a one-person "phone call," Nick gave new directions, and they got out at an Eddie Bauer store. Walking through the store and out a side entrance, with a three-block walk, they were home. After her sweep and the usual kitchen greeting and sounds, Mom was back for the Milk-Bone.

"That was an educational outing. You did not seem enamored with being called 'it.'"

"Rrcrunchrf."

"I did hear your attempt at a snore while Williams and I were talking, which was a nice touch."

"Woof."

Nick returned to the pictures and checked them against his memory. He thought one could be the follower from the tower, though having seen him only from long-distance glimpses, he could not be certain. Taking his time, Nick went through the pictures, committing all to memory until he was sure that he would recognize any he might encounter. Reading the background information was like reading the fine print under the photos displayed at the post office: stories of rapes, thefts, and murders, with a token white-collar swindler or two. Overall, an impressive group of choirboys operating under newly minted identities. He knew what that was like.

"Woof."

"I didn't say anything."

"Wrrff."

"Do you want to go see Helen about dinner?"

"Woof."

The aroma du jour was sage, and Helen was chopping vegetables on the block. "Could you handle grilled halibut and vegetables, or would you prefer hot dogs?"

"I wouldn't want you to go to all the trouble of boiling water, so why don't we stick with the fish."

"Humor from the weak minded is not usually funny."

"I will have to take your word for that."

"You are impossible."

"Mostly."

"Woof."

The fish was delicious—a good choice—and Nick was almost finished when his phone began the ring sequence. "Are we on camera?" he asked around the last mouthful as he headed upstairs to take the call.

"So they had you in their grasp and foolishly allowed you to escape," the rabbi said.

"Yep, and Williams believed that Mom is old and slow, barely able to get around."

"I take it he bought your cornpone act."

"I laid it on pretty thick, worked in a couple of 'Gods,' and Mom even faked a little snore."

"We might as well find a little humor where we can because the situation is becoming less amusing by the hour. This hacked e-mail drip and the monopoly of news cycles is having the effect of a seemingly hypnotized core of supporters being unencumbered by reality. All the pep rallies, call-and-response chants, bumper-sticker mottos, and stupid made-in-China hats are tiring. We are seeing many campaign people with ties to Russian business dealings, including the candidate. Several of the top staff have had multiple meetings with the Russian ambassador to the United States, who for decades has been known as their top spymaster and recruiter. While denying these documented contacts, by talking to him at all they are being worked in some way, usually unaware. All the hacking and leaks along with the fake news stories are part of an effort to disrupt this election and help this candidate. We know there is a bigger picture that we have hints of but are not seeing yet, but we must. This Williams does not strike me as important, someone on the inside. We see him as low-level staff looking for a paycheck, having no sensitive information about real campaign strategies or goals."

"Yes," Nick said. "He is only a stepping-stone to the real players. The good news is that he bought my act and invited me to a cocktail party tomorrow evening to meet more campaign people."

"That sounds like a good piece of work, and with enough cocktails, they could provide more insight than intended."

"Is it too cynical to imagine that a much larger donation might have had a more important initial contact person?" Nick asked.

"With this group, 'too cynical' is impossible. With each outrageous statement and blatant lie not being called out, they are more emboldened, calculating that they can get away with anything. We must redouble our efforts and examine every move in relation to their overall agenda, which, thankfully, we are aware of. Were the pictures helpful?"

"Yes. From the pictures, I have identified a Russian from my Starbucks visit who followed us after the meeting. We turned a corner, got into the only cab to be seen, and were gone, giving no indication of being aware of his presence. Tomorrow I will need one of the off-the-books plain-Jane vans you have access to and a medical interrogation kit. I will need the van to be on the ground floor of the parking garage two blocks south of the tower for tomorrow evening. I don't like working without the best possible intel, and I do not allow myself to be followed. After they lost us today, we will most likely be trailed again from the cocktail party, at which point we will go proactive, which is all I will say now. Tomorrow will be interesting."

"OK, I will handle your equipment request. This party should be informative to gauge how well your story holds up with a larger, more sophisticated audience."

"You don't sound very reassuring."

"What is reassuring is knowing that Mom will be along to extricate you from any sticky situation that you may blunder into." With that vote of confidence and a "happy hunting," the call ended.

Dressed in night gear, both black, they took different routes to the park, staying in alleys and shadows, seeing nothing noteworthy along the way. In the usual wooded area, they had a long training/exercise session. On the return route, they skirted the tower from a block away and saw the familiar congregation of security patrolling with the same strength as the day shift. Twenty-four-hour protection evidently meant just that. They skirted the well-lit high-traffic areas and arrived home without incident.

The next morning, the breakfast menu was back to oatmeal, fruit, yogurt, toast, and coffee. After breakfast, a messenger delivered a sealed packet containing keys and a picture of the van, as well as the medical inter-rogation kit, which included restraints, hoods, syringes, and several medications. The note explained that the van would be in the requested place by two o'clock. At two thirty, they were in character, finding the van on the ground floor, backed into an end space, easily accessible, and out of view of cameras. With the basic anonymous look of the countless work vans in the city, the only distin-guishing features were the magnetic plumbing company signs that could be removed easily. The bottom half of the vehicle was splattered with mud, making the license plates unreadable. Nick quickly arranged the kit inside, spread out for easy access, and they were on their way back home.

"How about I warm up what's left of the bisque before it spoils?" Helen asked.

"Good plan, and maybe there will be a bit extra for a kibble dribble."

"Very clever, Longfellow, and I will allow you to do the dribbling, which you seem suited for."

Soon it was show-time. Nick and Mom took the slow walk to the tower and through the busy lobby. Williams was at the door of the private room, where he greeted Nick and invited him in, Mom invisible in her white outfit, as usual.

"Thank you, Gene," said Nick, shaking hands and looking around. "You have a big crowd, and I'm glad you are here because I don't know anyone else."

"We can fix that. Would you like a drink?"

"Maybe a ginger ale. What I really need is to get off my feet," Nick told him.

Finding an empty table near the door, Williams introduced his helper, Jane, who went for the ginger ale. Nick sat with a sigh, and Mom leaned on his leg under the table and lay down in her invisible mode as Jane brought the ginger ale. The room was almost full; the guests were predominantly men, all enjoying cocktails and bar food brought by blond hostesses scattered throughout. Williams excused himself and headed across the room and returned with a smooth-looking man in a shiny suit.

"Mr. Hawkins, I would like you to meet Pete Manfred, our campaign manager. Pete, this is Mr. John Hawkins."

"Nice to meet you, sir," Nick said in his flat voice.

"The pleasure is mine," said Manfred. "We are thankful for all our supporters, especially generous ones like you and your PAC, who have been on board almost from the beginning."

"Well, that is very kind. We farmers can sometimes be a little slow, or we might have been in from the start," said Nick, testing a subtle defensiveness.

Manfred took the bait. "I meant no criticism, sir. Gene has filled me in about your group, and we are very happy with your involvement."

"Thank you, but it is true that we can be slow at times. You look familiar. Have you been in the papers recently about Asia or someplace?"

Manfred flinched slightly, recovered, and answered modestly, "I helped some officials over in Ukraine with a small matter that got some press coverage back here."

"That must be it. I don't recall any details of the story, just your name and picture. It is exciting to meet someone famous," Nick stroked.

"I hardly think of myself as famous, but thank you," he said.

Nick let stand the belief that a slow-witted farmer could not recall details of a story he had seen.

"Hey, have you met General Finegan, our security adviser?" Manfred asked.

"Do you mean General Michael Finegan, the toughest general we have seen in a long time?"

"The one and only. He just arrived, and you should meet him," said Manfred, waving Finegan to their table. "General Finegan, this is Mr. John Hawkins of that farming PAC that has been so supportive. Mr. Hawkins, General Finegan."

Shaking hands, Nick assumed an "aw shucks" attitude. "This is quite a party, meeting famous people and war heroes in the same room." Nick could tell from the glances and expressions that he was being seen exactly as he wanted—as an unimpressive country bumpkin. "I know you fellers are real busy, but if you ever have time, I would love to hear how you can manage such a complicated enterprise. If there was something I could understand and tell our group about, we might be able to get even more involved." Nick felt that since they were buying his act, he should try pushing things along, thinking they could not resist the smell of more donations.

"That sounds like a good idea," Manfred said with a nod from Finegan. "We have to get moving now but could meet up on Monday afternoon if you would be available."

"I will gladly make myself available," Nick said.

"Good. Let's say two o'clock here, and we will see you then."

"It's a date," Nick said awkwardly. They shook hands before Manfred left.

Nick and Mom stayed for a while with Williams, who made a few more introductions, including to one of the blond hostesses, Shirley, who was pretty and looking bored. When Nick asked if she was a New York native, she told him, "Born and bred, NYU, design school, grad school, and now a successful political hostess."

Nick caught the ruefulness and asked, "Do you know which art galleries I should see while I am here?"

"There are so many, I would need to know about your interests to make a recommendation. I must look busy now, but here is my card. You can give me a call, and we can discuss it."

"Great. I will do that, and thanks."

"Good. I will talk to you later." And she was gone, joining a full table of drinkers, the professional smile back in place.

"Gene, I am running out of steam, so best be going. Thanks for the invite and letting me meet some of the famous people you work with."

"No problem, Mr. Hawkins. See you Monday."

"I look forward to it. See you then."

As Nick and Mom got up slowly and left, Mom was still ignored. Walking from the tower in the opposite direction from home, they again stopped frequently to look in store windows and rest. After a few stops, Nick had identified two followers: one a tall man from the table Shirley had joined, the other a short, stocky one on the opposite side of the street, hanging farther back.

"We have fish on," he told Mom.

"Rrrwoof."

With a longer stop for window shopping, the closest follower had to backtrack to keep his distance with his comrade doing the same. Now with the needed distance from their followers, they turned into the garage and hustled to the van. Opening the side door, away from the street entrance, Nick pulled off the shabby-suit costume, leaving him in his all-black exercise outfit, pulling up his hood with the mask. Then, with Mom's white long-legged sweater zipped off, along with the vest and muzzle, the black dog was ready for work. With their signals acknowledged, Mom crept behind a car and crouched, ready. Soon the closest tail entered the garage and, seeing no one, moved in slowly, looking in cars as he passed. As he came past the van, Nick worked around the back, out of sight, until the man was past the front. As the chaser hesitated to look at the van side, Nick quickly stepped around the front end and delivered a powerful ridge hand to the carotid artery in the neck, which staggered the man. Then, with a left hook to the temple, the guy crumpled and was out. Nick opened the side door and hefted him inside, where he shackled hands and feet, put a black hood over his head, and administered a hypodermic dose of George Washington (the "I cannot tell a lie" concoction). As he stepped out and closed the door, the shorter chaser rounded the front of the van, holding an ugly pistol with a silencer. In the next instant, Mom had the gun hand in her jaws, and Nick heard bones snapping as the gun hit the floor, and the man yelped. In a blur, Mom now had him face down with jaws clamped on the back of his neck. Without a word. Nick plunged a needle into the exposed neck, and the man lay still. Nick put him into the van next to his partner, applied the restraints and hood, picked up the gun, and closed the door. Then, after putting on both of their costumes, Nick locked the van, and they were on their way. After the dialing routine, the rabbi was on the line. "I wondered when you would call. What is your situation?"

"We have two informants waiting for your driver. One probably Russian, the other undetermined. We had no trouble, thanks to Mom. We will continue our stroll home. Our friends are not talking, not even moving. They seem to be asleep."

"Excellent. The driver is very close and will have them in the recruitment office quickly. Good work, and give your boss an extra Milk-Bone when you get inside. You two need to get seen again—the sooner, the better, so you are not on the missing list. Maybe even a walk back past the tower."

"That is the plan, and we can do a full debrief when we are home."

"Later then." Click.

"Let's get out of here; there are Milk-Bones waiting."

"Woof."

After an uneventful walk past the tower, the security, and the cameras, the old, limping man with the white service dog was unremarkable and slowly meandered home unfollowed. Passing the Milk-Bones, Nick said, "This next debriefing will be interesting."

"Woof."

Chapter 9

●　　●　　●

BUY INTO THE CAMPAIGN, PLANT THE STING SEED

After the excitement of the night's escapade in the parking garage, Nick was sound asleep when the phone rang, and he awakened to the clicks and buzzes. His watch said four thirty, and it took him a moment to realize that it was morning. Then his rabbi was speaking.

"You are associating with some really nasty people. These guys are both Russian, part of a diplomatic security department that we have been watching for months. They are tasked with surveilling anyone contacting the candidate or campaign staff, and their playbook includes all your actions and more. This is the same outfit that attempted, and thought they succeeded at, destroying the *Veritas* and all crew aboard. The only information they had about Hawkins was his representation of the PAC. This was a normal procedure to follow a campaign worker, a donor, or both home and trace any contacts they could discover. There are no indications that your cover is suspect. After 'debriefing,' this pair were administered a cocktail that erases any memory of the previous twenty-four hours and indicates a high alcohol level. Sometime today, a cleaning-staff member will discover them in a private room at an exclusive gay nightclub. Incidentally, one had a mangled hand with broken bones and tooth marks. We did not treat the broken bones but were able to disguise the tooth marks with some other cuts and scrapes. There were two pistols with silencers, which are being tested for comparisons with unsolved shootings here and abroad. Reporting to their supervisor could prove challenging for them. Nice work, though I am unsure who did the heavy lifting: you or your boss."

"Well, good morning to you too, and my boss always has my back."

"Looks like she saved your butt also."

"Woof." Of course, Mom was wide awake and listening.

"The campaign news shows that the hacked e-mail releases and fake news are having the desired effect and, impossible as it may seem, we are predicting a dead heat election. If this trend continues or if there is a last-minute surprise, which the candidate is hinting at, then there will be an upset victory. I am messengering more data. Have a nice breakfast." Click.

"That was informative. Why don't we have a walk and then see if your friend in the kitchen is up for feeding us?"

"Woof."

They were soon at the park, in character, Mom sporting the sweater, muzzle, and vest. It was still dark, with sparse traffic and few people about, and they had a vigorous workout in the wooded area and an uneventful walk home.

The offer of eggs Benedict sounded good, and Nick would surely be appraising the hollandaise sauce. Mom was particular about her kibble, primarily in terms of quantity.

"Helen, that was excellent and the hollandaise perfect."

"Ah, the heathen has a small degree of culture."

"I so appreciate an exchange of compliments, even an underhanded one. I would love to stay and banter, but duty calls. Mom can stay and fill you in on our adventures while I work," he said before heading upstairs.

"She has enough culture for you both."

I cannot win with this one, Nick thought to himself.

With the ring, buzzes, and clicks again, the rabbi was speaking. "Just a couple more points. Comparing data from phone intercepts and other sources, we see a strict adherence to the agenda outlined in del Mundo's found package. When the candidate switched the rhetoric from 'crooked Mildred' to 'the election is rigged,' we knew that the fix was in, their rigging successful.

"Can you check with del Mundo to see if his modifications are complete and ready to travel? There will soon be a messenger packet with more intel and detail that you will find helpful. Later." Click.

Using the scrambled sat phone, Nick went right to work and was speaking with del Mundo within minutes. "Professor, how are you, and how goes your reconfiguration?"

"Hi, Nick, nice to hear from you. Figured you would call given the state of things. We are finishing up the final paintwork after disguising the *Veritas* once again. This time, it is a vintage megayacht with a midnight-blue hull, brilliant-white top sides, and a foreign registration as *Bubble*. We have altered its propulsion systems and now have a different sonar profile. There were enough changes to the doghouse configuration for a very different visual appearance, and the fishing skiffs were traded for water toys and a pair of plushed-out launches. Below decks, we have augmented our electronic capabilities and have issued proper yacht whites for the crew. We are stocked, fueled, and ready for travel when the paint is dry, which should be sometime tonight."

"That's good. We need you on station in NYC ASAP, so it's good that you are ready. Please send Steiger home if you haven't already done so. He will need distance from us for his security as well as for providing West Coast eyes and ears, possibly a media voice."

"Very good idea, and we will advise you of our itinerary and schedule. It sounds like we will be talking in person soon."

"Good. You will not be here a moment too soon. All haste and safe sailing."

"Roger, out."

The report that the *Bubble* would soon be nearby was welcome news to Nick, especially after the parking-garage incident. While the followers becoming armed attackers was alarming, the prospect of del Mundo with Smith, Jones, and Black being nearby was reassuring.

After the calls, the messenger arrived with a thick package. Nick delved into it along with the picture files. The package detailed more Russian involvement with campaign staff and that the depth of disinformation had more than half the reports on TV networks and social media being fake news. The propaganda attack was flourishing to great effect. Also outlined was a high-end real estate "opportunity" that could be used as a trap for the Russians and campaign money laundering schemes that Nick should mention if his meeting was going smoothly.

Nick was restless and hungry when Helen asked if a picnic supper of franks, beans, and potato salad would be tolerable. He told her that the meal would suit his mood and needs.

"I knew you were a simple man at heart," she said.

"How did you become so perceptive?"

"It is difficult to obscure the obvious."

Nick left that alone and enjoyed the supper, especially the freshly made potato salad.

Mom enjoyed her kibble as always, and they were soon in black and out for a night recon run. Staying a block from the tower, they found a good viewpoint and saw increased activity. Security appeared to be of the same strength, but the influx of people being dropped off and picked up later by limos was virtually nonstop.

"Looks like somebody poked a stick in the hornet's nest."

"Rruff."

Nick wondered if he was the cause of the extra traffic or if there were more crises afoot. He knew there would be much to learn at tomorrow's meeting. With a long, circuitous route home at a fast pace, they arrived. Mom did the sweep, and then there were the kitchen sounds, Milk-Bone, and sleep time. After returning from the morning walk in character, Nick got into the messenger file again. With seemingly daily revelations of so many campaign officials with ties to Russians, a staff shake-up was anticipated, and Hawkins would probably be dealing with different people. His first meeting agenda point was to make sure there was no suspicion about his cover. There was detail about the propaganda techniques being used, such as weaponizing the release of hacked e-mails to trolls and bots flooding news and social media outlets, compromising of wealthy or influential individuals with bribes and/or threats, and the overriding theme of laundering money stolen from national treasuries by autocratic leaders and oligarchs. The memo emphasized the importance of focusing on the Russians, not the candidate, who could become an expendable fall guy, leaving the Russians in the clear.

The ranch sting would involve a forty-thousand-acre big-game hunting resort in Texas owned by one of the PAC members who anticipated some near future estate issues. This five-star resort was booked solid for years in advance, had domestic and African game animals, and had an appraised value approaching $250 million. The story was that it could be purchased for slightly more than half value for a cash sale. The packet also contained an envelope with a cashier's-check donation for the campaign, which should be given before the hint of the ranch deal. This was a big intel dump to process, but Nick understood the logic and thought this sting could appear too juicy to be ignored.

"We have a full plate for our meeting, and a plate for lunch would be good about now," he told Mom.

"Woof."

Fortified with clam chowder and sourdough biscuits and kibble, they were ready for show-time.

Moving slowly, in character, they entered the lobby, which was more crowded than it had been before. The bar was almost full, with men and women conversing in several languages, including Russian, and tension in the air was almost palpable. Williams opened the meeting-room door with a friendly greeting. "Mr. Hawkins, good to see you, come in. Coffee?"

"Yes, hello, Gene, thanks. Where is everybody?"

"We will be joined shortly—apologies, a previous meeting went long."

"No problem. I am ready to sit and rest my feet," Nick told him, following Mom as she crawled under her table of choice. He sat and took a sip of the coffee.

A few minutes later, two men joined Williams, and they came to the table.

"Mr. Hawkins, I would like you to meet Mr. Ron Prescott, our new campaign manager, and Mr. Sam Bandini, our new security adviser. Gentlemen, Mr. John Hawkins of the Strong Leaders PAC."

"It is nice to meet you both. No offense, but what happened to the folks I met last week?" Nick asked.

"We have taken steps to avoid complications from some Democrats' partisan demonizing of past business relationships," Prescott said.

"Sounds like heading them off at the pass," Nick chuckled.

"That pretty much sums it up," said Bandini.

"Well, judging from the poll numbers I see on the news, it looks like the campaign is in good hands," Nick said. "We had some concerns hearing the candidate say that the election is rigged."

"The e-mails proved that the Democratic primary was rigged, but we have taken steps to ensure a different result in the general election," Prescott said with a smug smile.

Nick picked up an attitude of certainty with no trace of doubt. "That is good news. We farmers have been worried about four more years like the last eight and are counting on a change. Our question now is whether the situation is under control to the point that further donations are not needed or accepted."

With a glance at Bandini, Prescott said, "Like they say in sports, it's not over until it's over. We have a way to go and are still looking for funding."

"Like I said before, we need this change and would like to offer more support. We have all pitched in, and I have brought a cashier's check," said Nick, handing over the envelope. He could see Prescott struggling, wanting to look at the check but finally pocketing the unopened envelope.

With Prescott taking time to explain details of the campaign organization and inner workings, Nick asked several questions and appeared overwhelmed by the answers. He needed clarifications of many processes that would have been obvious to a more sophisticated person.

Dragging out this discussion to the point of making the campaign operatives visibly restless, Nick felt that it was time to plant the seed. Looking at his watch, he said, "Golly, look at what time it is. I didn't mean to take up so much of your day explaining things to a dumb farmer. You are very patient, and I should be going and let you fellers get back to your good work. By the way, one of our members has a large hunting ranch he needs to sell quickly to settle some family issues. His urgency could leave room for a large profit. This is way beyond my means, and I probably shouldn't have even mentioned it, but I realize you folks might bump into some high rollers." Standing up slowly, shifting a little, trying for sheepish, Nick quietly waited.

"We do know some real estate people, obviously. What kind of property is this again?"

Still looking sheepish, Nick said, "This is a hunting ranch of forty thousand acres with domestic and imported big-game animals. It's a five-star resort with full facilities that is booked years in advance. It could probably be purchased on a cash deal for roughly half the appraised value. I am sorry to take your time from your real business; you must hear thousands of stories. Anyhow, keep up the good work, and let's win this one because our country really needs this candidate."

Shaking hands again, Nick had to bite back a smile as Prescott told him, "We might know someone who could help your friend. Thank you and your group for your generous support. We must get back to work now. Maybe we could have lunch tomorrow or the next day when we are not so pressed for time and you have had time for what we discussed to sink in. Gene here will contact you." Prescott and Bandini left.

"You are working with some real smart people," he told Williams.

"I am glad they impressed you. I have your card and will call you with the lunch plans, and thank you again."

"Good seeing you again, Gene, thanks." Nick slowly left, the still-invisible Mom at his side.

Walking from the tower with the frequent rest stops and window shopping, Nick saw no followers. They had two cab rides, changed directions, and walked through a hotel lobby and sporting-goods store before going home. After a sweep and a Milk-Bone, Mom settled down for a short nap as Nick dialed. Then the clicks and buzzes, and the rabbi was on the line.

"Are you home or a hostage?" he asked.

"Home, with no parade today. I did have the pleasure of meeting the new campaign manager and security adviser. Williams is still the chief flunky, no surprise. There was no mention of missing security people or hint of suspicion of me. They made lame explanations of the staff change and had a tough time pocketing the donation envelope without checking the amount. After boring them with dumb questions about campaign workings, I mentioned the possible ranch deal, of which they said maybe they knew someone and would get back to me over lunch in the next couple of days. They were smugly confident about the election. Del Mundo is finishing up work on the boat and should be in motion tonight, so barring any major hurricanes, he should be on post here within a week."

"That all sounds good. Their response to the ranch deal will inform our next moves either way. We are moving a step at a time and must link the steps in the direction we need. Let me know when the next meet is scheduled." Clicks, and the rabbi was gone.

After a slow start, the battle was becoming more intense, and the need to catch up to the action was crucial. With possibilities, combinations, and details running circles in his head, Nick eventually fell into an exhausted sleep.

Chapter 10

⬤　⬤　⬤

SET THE STAGE, NURTURE THE SEED

Waking up rested after a solid seven hours of uninter-rupted sleep, Nick was looking at Mom's expectant face close to the bed. "You are looking at me with that hungry, reproachful expression. Have I slept past kibble time or something?"

"Woof."

The morning walk and exercise in the park were uneventful and refreshing. With the blood pumping, Nick had a few ideas, which he began analyzing on the walk home. After Mom's sweep and Milk-Bone, Nick used the sat phone to contact del Mundo. "Professor, hello. Are you in motion with the dry paint?"

"Yes, Nick, good morning. We were moving shortly after our talk and will be through the canal today. With the configuration and propulsion modifications, our cruising speed has increased significantly. There are no major storms on the radar, and we will be on station much sooner than anticipated. What can I do for you?"

"Since you are cruising smoothly and Merrit and the crew are capable of running the boat, would you be able to help with some research?" Nick asked.

"Of course. This is good timing. What are we talking about?"

"I need to contact one of the contractors who filed a lawsuit against the tower for nonpayment, specifically the mechanical contractor. I am also looking for contact with the building-maintenance company."

"It sounds as if there could be surreptitious activity on the horizon."

"Isn't that a normal horizon in our world? This could be important for a successful counterstrategy."

"Coming from you, I presumed this would not be a flippant request. I am at my screens now and will be back to you soon." Del Mundo went to work.

Nick was immersed in the rabbi's packet when his phone rang, clicked, and buzzed.

"Nick," the rabbi said, "fasten your seat belt because the surprise is forthcoming. The FBI director is going to release a statement revealing a separate e-mail trove hacked from a Democratic congressman he says could prove incriminating to Mildred. There are no details or specifics. This close to the vote, there will be substantial effect. We see this as a tipping point, which will transform a close election into an upset that has never seemed possible. We are adjusting our strategy to this presumptive result, and our timetable is also changing."

"I am not surprised, as the campaign appeared satisfied and confident—like the cat that ate the canary. We do have del Mundo moving at full speed and doing research relating to a plan of action I am developing. I will update you on this and will adjust my thinking to what will soon be our new reality."

"Good. We can discuss this as it develops. Now the meeting about the ranch deal will be even more important. Got to go, talk soon."

The sat phone squawked, and del Mundo was speaking. "I am sending you contact info for three contractors, all who have been stiffed by the candidate and are disgruntled. Livid might be a more accurate description of their attitudes."

"Let's hope livid will translate into motivated. I will need clandestine assistance for my plan to work," Nick said.

"OK, I am sending now. Out."

The important profile was of Bob Johnson, the mechanical contractor, a Marine Corps veteran who had built his company from scratch into one of the most respected contractors in the city. Although he handled large-scale projects, his company was really a mom-and-pop operation, and the $400,000 he had not been paid had him stretched to make his payroll commitments. Nick thought these circumstances made Johnson a good prospect for the assistance he would require.

Connecting with the rabbi, after the clicks and buzzes, he explained what he had in mind and heard no objection. He asked which persona he should use for meeting the contractor. They decided that he should appear without the Hawkins disguise and be an agent of a secret letter agency. The rabbi would messenger him an official-looking ID and badge, and a Marine Corps contact person would vouch for Nick. For this action, Nick would be Neil Miller.

Calling the business office, he was quickly routed to Johnson. "Hello, Mr. Johnson. My name is Neil Miller, and I am with an agency familiar with your lawsuit for nonpayment. Our group stays under the radar, so you have probably never heard of us. We believe we may be able to help your situation and think you could help us also. I would like to meet with you in person to discuss this. I will give you a name with a number at the Marine Corps who will confirm my status. This involves a matter of national security that, as a veteran and patriot, I am certain you will support. Please verify my credentials with the Corps. I will call you back in one hour so we can set a meeting, and thank you for your service."

Hanging up, Nick was sure the rabbi's man at the corps would accomplish the task, and so began the site selection for the meet. One hour later, Johnson answered the phone and was agreeable and sounded ready to meet. Nick told him of a small park near the river and confirmed that eight o'clock would be good. They would meet at a fountain and then walk and talk. With the schedule set, Nick returned to the files and research and received the messenger packet within the hour. He thought the ID and badge looked good, and the accompanying dossier on Johnson was thorough and helpful.

With Nick in black night gear and Mom in her natural black with a black service vest, it was a fast walk through alleys and shadows, and they found Johnson at the fountain. After introducing himself, shaking hands, and showing his credentials, Nick was pleased when Johnson asked him who his sidekick was. He introduced Mom, who got a pat and a sniff of Johnson, whom she awarded a rare approval.

"I've got a couple of shepherds at home, and she probably smells them," he said.

"She likes dog lovers and seems to find no objection to you, which is a good recommendation," Nick said. As they walked and talked, Nick found himself liking the former marine and felt sympathetic to his plight, impressed that he was no victim but a fighter.

"I have taken a loan to pay my employees and my attorney's retainer. I do quality work and never overcharge my customers, and I don't care how rich someone is, I will not lie down and be cheated. A contract is a contract, and I delivered as promised. I am not the only one being stiffed, but I may be the one with the best court case. So how do we help each other?"

"To begin, our group is familiar with your law firm, having been involved with it on previous cases. It is among the best and most honorable. With your help, we will be able to tap a special fund and significantly reduce your legal fees. The attorneys have always been cooperative, and the merits of your case combined with your background make this an easy call. What we need from you are the blueprints and schematics along with details of systems and equipment. We are also interested in speaking with the building's maintenance company and hope you can provide us with a contact there. Our involvements with both companies will remain classified with security enforced. We are not new to this type of clandestine relationship, so you will be well protected with no blowback. Can you help?"

"I will be more than happy to help and can have copies of plans and schematics for you first thing tomorrow. Regarding the maintenance company, Universal Maintenance happens to be owned and operated by Joey Corbone, my wife's second cousin and a close family friend. If he thinks it will help me, he will do just about anything you ask, especially if you give him protection."

"This does sound like a lucky break."

"I could say the same. At this point, I can use all the help I can find," Johnson said.

"Good. I will send a messenger to your office in the morning, and if you could call Mr. Corbone and, with his permission, put his contact info in the messenger packet, I will contact him. We will cause no liability for you and, for your protection, share no details of our actions. We will provide similar protection for Mr. Corbone and his company. We are grateful for your patriotism, and we will enjoy contributing to a positive outcome of your legal battle. Thank you, and you should see the messenger, who will show credentials, around eleven o'clock." Nick said good-bye as Mom gave a little wiggle, and they were gone.

"Did you like that guy?"

"Woof."

"You sure can spot a dog lover."

"Woof."

Back home, with Mom's sweep and Milk-Bone and the Helen sounds, a delicious smell was coming from the kitchen.

"I hope you like lasagna because that is dinner with a salad and bread," Helen said.

"It does smell pretty good."

"If you really have no smart remarks, we may dine."

Nick dug in silently. Mom crunched.

After sleep, the morning walk in character, home for the sweep, Milk-Bone, and time studying the intel packets, the messenger arrived. The plans were complete and gave Nick a good overview of the tower construction and systems with detail enough to outline the steps they would need to take. Also included was the contact information for Corbone, which was his first call.

On the first ring, Joey Corbone answered in an upbeat voice.

"Mr. Corbone, my name is Neil Miller, and Bob Johnson referred you. He said you could be trusted and that I should talk with you."

"Yes, Bob called me last night after meeting with you. He did not elaborate but said you were with a secret agency and could use our help. I am a veteran and a patriot and am always willing to help my country, though I have no idea what this is about or what I could do," Corbone said.

"That is how these things often work. It would be best for us to meet to discuss the matter. I imagine you have a full schedule. Could we have a short get-together this evening?"

"That would be best, as my schedule is full all day. After seven o'clock would be possible for me."

"We could meet at eight o'clock at the small park where I met Mr. Johnson last night."

"Yes, that is fine. Bob told me about the fountain. Sounds kind of cloak-and-dagger and all that stuff. I know the park and can be there at eight."

"Good. See you then."

After much studying, strategy gaming, and a light supper, Nick and Mom repeated the stealthy route to the park and found Corbone at the fountain.

"Hello, Mr. Corbone, I am Neil Miller, and thank you for taking time to meet with me. Mr. Johnson had good things to say about you."

"Nice to meet you, Mr. Miller, and who is your lovely friend?"

"This is my boss. Meet Mr. Corbone."

With another rare approval, Mom gave a little wiggle and accepted a brief ear scratch with a "You're a pretty girl."

"I was in the army and learned that chain of command is critical. It's nice to see that you are in good shape in that regard." He laughed.

Nick gave a little chuckle. "It's true, but we can't be too effusive with praise, or it might go to her head."

"It's just nice when we all know who is in charge."

Nick felt comfortable with Corbone and got right to the matter at hand. "As I explained to Mr. Johnson, I am with a low-key letter agency, and we are dealing with a situation that presents a threat to our national security, to our democracy itself. Mr. Johnson is very helpful, and we will reciprocate with assistance in resolving his problem. We are happy that your company has not found itself in the same position. Our discussions and actions, if any, will be classified top secret and treated accordingly, with no exceptions. If you choose to help with our efforts, the only thing I can promise in return is the gratitude and goodwill of our nation. Should I continue?"

"Yes, please do. As a patriot, this goodwill has meaning, and if I can help Bob by helping you, then I am all for it. What can I do?"

"In the coming weeks, we would like to provide you with two or three temporary employees for the tower maintenance. These men will all have documented qualifications and work histories, and we can backdate their applications for your files. They will be needed for a short period, seven to ten days. These temporary personnel additions can be justified by new service protocols, sick leave of regulars, or both. We will pay for salaries of any displaced employees with small bonuses. You and your employees will have no knowledge of our activities, and we will guarantee that none of you will be in any position of liability, either personally or corporately. Your company and the company or companies you have contracts with will appear to be aggrieved parties joined in the same position. Any inquiries into our people will leave you harmless and will lead nowhere. This is a sensitive operation that involves a serious threat to our national security."

"This does sound serious, even ominous. I am willing to help, but I wonder if I should consult my attorney."

"Of course, but remember that this is a classified matter, so your discussion would have to be made in the context of lawyer-client confidentiality. If you happen to use the same law firm as Mr. Johnson, then this will be easier, as we have worked with the lawyers previously, and they are accustomed to classified matters and are dependable allies."

"That does simplify things because I have known these lawyers for a long time and steered Bob to them," Corbone said.

Nick had already learned this from del Mundo's file but said, "That is good news. Why don't you first talk with them? Then, if you are reassured, we can proceed."

"I can do that. I am thinking that this has some urgency, so I will get with them tomorrow if possible. My schedule is adjustable, and as long as they are not stuck in court all day, then I'm sure they can find a few minutes for me."

"Good. Thank you. You can contact me at this number when you have their blessing." Nick gave Corbone a small note with a number that would route through the committee switchboard to his phone. Shaking hands again, Nick said, "Good meeting you, and thanks for your consideration."

"I hope I can help, and nice meeting you both." That earned him a little Mom wiggle.

Walking away, Nick said, "Are you feeling well? That is two approvals in two days."

"Who woof."

After the morning routine, Nick's phone rang and Williams was speaking and asked Mr. Hawkins if he could meet at three o'clock at the tower. "Sure, Gene, what's up?"

"One of our associates might have interest in your friend's ranch and would like to learn more about it," Williams said.

"This is a surprise, but sure. Where?"

"The small meeting room off the lobby bar will be fine," Williams said.

"Good, thanks. See you there."

As if on cue, his phone rang again with clicks, buzzes, and the rabbi. "How are you progressing?" he asked.

"Pretty well so far," Nick said. "The mechanical contractor, Johnson, is good, a veteran, a patriot, and motivated. Being stiffed on his contract with the tower has pushed his company to the verge of bankruptcy. He does not appreciate being ripped off and is pissed. He provided me with blueprints, schematics, and an intro to his wife's cousin, Joey Corbone, the maintenance contractor, who by a nice coincidence is also a veteran and good friend of the Johnson family. They both use the same law firm, with whom we have always had good rapport. He, too, wants to help, and we have promised them both no blowback, which though possibly tricky is not as much as several past exploits. The capper is that Mom approved of them both."

"Your judgment is sound, but Mom's approval seals the deal."

"Thanks, we don't want to confuse the chain of command. The other development is a three o'clock meeting with Williams and a supposed associate interested in the ranch."

"That is progress. Do you need anything for this meeting?"

"I am reviewing the files and brochure and am OK, but I will call if there are any questions."

"Good luck."

The brochure was well done, the land enormous, the structures elegant and comfortable, and the array of game animals, domestic and imported, impressive. A luxury killing zoo, he mused.

His phone rang, and Corbone said he had just left the office of his attorney, who told him that the group was solid and always covered its helpers. He said he was in and asked what was next. Nick told him that he was working on research and planning and thought they should meet in a few days. Corbone said he was looking forward to their talk.

Back to the ranch file, Nick thought he had a good grasp of the facility, the story, and the strategy. He wondered who the potential buyer was and figured that this meeting would be with a proxy for the actual principles involved. He would make no assumptions and be prepared for any possibilities.

After a last-minute review of his notes, Nick was in character and walked with Mom into the busy lobby.

Williams opened the door and met Nick with a hand-shake and a friendly smile. "Come in, Mr. Hawkins, it's nice to see you."

"Good to see you, Gene. You must be very busy as usual."

"Always, but never too busy for a loyal supporter. You remember Mr. Bandini, and this is Mr. Sergei Korsikov, an associate of ours."

Shaking hands with both, Nick said, "Good seeing you again, Mr. Bandini, and a pleasure to meet you, Mr. Korsikov."

With nods and smiles all around, they sat, Mom already under the table, invisible but alert beneath the tired-dog act.

"I have told Mr. Korsikov what little I know about the ranch. Maybe we could begin with your filling in some details."

"Yes, of course," said Nick, handing over the brochure. "This will probably be much more informative than listening to a simple farmer and teacher stumbling through a description."

Watching them peruse the brochure, Nick could tell that they were impressed despite their efforts to show no reaction. He quietly waited for them to speak.

"This is an impressive property," Bandini finally said with an accompanying nod from Korsikov. "Can you outline for us the reason and terms of the sale?"

"Certainly," said Nick. "The owner is dealing with a family issue and considers legal action a future possibility. He is a person who has strong conservative values and always seeks to avoid conflict. Even though it would involve a loss to sell quickly, he has decided that peace of mind has value. He would be willing to consider a cash sale much less than the appraised value. This would need to be finalized quickly to be legal and avoid any complications. I have no knowledge of the specific issues involved, only that closing a transaction within the tight time frame will prevent any liabilities or claims. I am not a lawyer, but I do know that he has competent legal counsel. I imagine that your due diligence will confirm all this."

"I suspect that we will confirm what you have said. What are the numbers, please?"

"You will need to negotiate the specifics, but my understanding is that the appraised value of the property is somewhere north of $250 million, and the bookings are a full two years out. I have heard unofficially that he would sell in the under $200million range. Again, these numbers are not definite but are probably in the real neighborhood."

"On the surface, this sounds tantalizing," Korsikov said. "We will, of course, do our diligence and, depending on those answers, and if positive, will need to meet again to know how to proceed. If our research does not prove positive, then it has been nice meeting you."

"That seems reasonable. Thank you all for your time, and I will await your call," Nick said, before standing.

"It has been our pleasure," Bandini said. "We must be going, but thank you for thinking of us."

After they left, Nick said, "Thanks again, Gene. My friend will be grateful if this pans out."

"It seems a good possibility. I must get to my next meeting, and thanks for mentioning this."

"I felt a little embarrassed for bringing it up, but now I don't feel so bad," Nick said.

"No worries. I'll let you know when I hear from them either way."

Mom was still invisible when Williams left.

"That was a cheery bunch."

"Ruff."

"I agree. They are a different type than our contractor friends."

"Woof."

With the slow walk, stopping for rest, and window shopping, there were no followers and still no mention of the last two. At home with the sweep and Helen sounds, Mom gulped the Milk-Bone and happily lay down to work on a real bone. Nick dialed and heard the clicks and buzzes and the voice of the rabbi.

"Have they allowed your escape again?"

"Yes, I am still in the clear, and Mom is still invisible. Bandini brought an 'associate' who calls himself Sergei Korsikov. I will be interested about what you can dig up about him. This was preliminary, restrained, and non-committal, and I left a brochure with them. As we surmised, the greed seems to have taken hold. On the other front, del Mundo is making good time and ahead of schedule. Our new allies, the contractors, are good to go, and I trust they have been vetted, which should confirm Mom's excellent nose. We might have some interesting times coming our way."

"Just how we like it," the rabbi said. "Keep me updated, and I will do the same."

Chapter 11

●　●　●

TRICK OUT THE RIDE, GET IN THE FRONT MAN'S FACE

The next day broke with a cloudy sky and hints of rain, and the morning walk was in half light. Back home, after the usual protocol, they had just started breakfast, Nick with bacon and eggs and Mom with kibble, when the sat phone squawked, and del Mundo started speaking. "Hey, Nick, we have been running high speed twenty-four-seven, no waiting at the canal, making good time, and should arrive by evening. We have arranged moorage at a commercial dock, where we will be mostly concealed by warehouses, barges, and a couple of tugs. We will be close to you, only a fast launch ride away."

"That is good news. We have more planning to do and will need to begin as soon as you arrive," Nick said.

"That's fine. I'll call when we are tied down and send the launch for you."

"We will be ready and waiting for your call."

Nick was almost finished rewarming his breakfast when he heard the clicks and buzzes and the rabbi on the line. "Good morning, Nick. We researched your man Korsikov, and you will be interested to know that he is a longtime Russian intelligence operative who is now in an undefined management position with Vnesheconombank. This is a Russian-owned bank with a New York branch that has had several employees deported or imprisoned after convictions of spying. Your boy Korsikov is part of the intelligence network and has close ties to oligarchs, including the 'aluminum king.' We will be interested in the method used to connect to the candidate, how he will approach the middleman function. We suspect the inherent large profit of the ranch deal will be too great to resist. What do you hear from del Mundo?"

"The *Bubble* is making good time, expected this evening, and we will begin planning immediately upon its arrival."

"Good. Talk to you soon."

Studying the tower plans, Nick looked for access points in the heating and air conditioning equipment and specifics of the elevators. This was an overview, noting potential areas and circuits that could be useful. Smith and Black, wizards in all phases of electronics and computer technology, would evaluate these. The engineers' combined expertise would determine which parts of the plan were viable and the mechanics of enacting them. The more prepared he was, the more able he would be to understand their assessments. The material was complex, and hours had passed when the sat phone squawked. "We are approaching the moorage and should be settled within the hour. The launch can pick you up at the Seventy-Ninth Street boat basin. I will call when the launch is thirty minutes from your pickup. Bring your flashlight, and use our three-two-one flash code for the launch, which will be laying off from the dock."

"Sounds good. See you soon."

Grabbing a quick sandwich and coffee, Nick rolled up the prints, secured the oversized tubes in his backpack, and fashioned a cover over the protruding ends. Watching this activity, Mom knew that an outing of some kind was approaching.

"Rruff."

"You are correct. We have work to do."

"Woof."

Soon the sat phone again squawked. Del Mundo said the *Bubble* was in place, and Nick told him they were on the move. Now in black night gear, they did a fast walk through alleys and shadows and arrived at the boat basin in fifteen minutes. Nick thought he could see the launch in the darkness and gave the flashes, which were answered by the shadow in the water that moved in to the dock. Smith and Jones greeted them as they hopped aboard. "Hi, Mom, nice to see you. Thanks for bringing your friend," said Smith. Mom, happy to see an old friend, wiggled and gave him a little lick.

"Nice to see you too," Nick said.

"Yes, glad you could make it."

Mom wiggled to Jones at the helm, and Nick, laughing, shook hands with both crew members.

The launch was moving as soon as Nick and Mom were on board. After a short ride out and around, they were alongside the *Bubble*, which showed only a slight resemblance to the *Veritas*.

"She looks good—maybe the best ever," Nick said.

"We like her, especially the increased speed and capabilities," Smith said.

On board, they greeted Merrit and found del Mundo and Black in the coms room. After the greeting and small talk, with Mom happily whining to more favorite friends, they got down to business. Nick spread out the plans and noted the areas he had thought interesting. Explaining what he had in mind, he saw wheels turning in their heads.

"The heat/AC ducts are probably a good starting point," del Mundo said. "Could they be used for access or integrated into electronic apparatus, or both?"

"If we could adapt miniature drones to the duct sizing, then we would have multiple options. We could install microcameras in the grills at specific locations. These could transmit real-time video feeds of targeted areas," Smith said.

"Establishing this type of surveillance capability would provide valuable intel that could help coordinate the encounter action and be valuable afterward," Nick said.

"That is correct," Black said, "and I don't see much difficulty with this piece. We can use proven existing technology to create these video streams. I think we could also connect all the ducting and outlet grills to audio receivers, virtually turning all the hardware into microphones. This system would allow us to record all sounds from the targeted video areas as well as surrounding spaces, such as halls and elevators."

"That is a nice segue, Mr. Black," Nick said, "which brings us to the next question: the site of the encounter. I initially considered the encounter in terms of a one-on-one situation, but maybe we should be thinking of a one-on-technology confrontation with a disguised identity and voice. You mentioned that an elevator would be an easily secured site, which might best serve our purpose."

"If you are asking if an elevator could be an easily secured temporary area," Smith said, "then the answer is yes. We would need further study of the plans, but this could be the most workable solution to the site question."

"OK, I think we have a possible framework for our logistical requirements. If we are agreed, I suggest we begin here to confirm that our technology and equipment applied to this specific location is viable and has a high probability of success," del Mundo said. "The next questions are the encounter messaging and means of delivery. In a controlled private environment, we could have delivery by personal encounter or by an anonymous audiovisual presentation."

"Since we are already decided about the message content, the question becomes the where, when, and how of the delivery," Black said. "Our research of the plans and equipment will likely inform our decisions about these questions."

"OK," del Mundo said, "we know the next task is research. Another question involves timing. If our research and equipment construction go quickly, then we could have the option of staging the encounter pre-election, which would be less problematic with candidate security. After the candidate becomes elected, we will surely see a significantly increased security level. We have only a week to finalize and stage the encounter for the pre-election timing to be an option."

"You are correct, Professor. We will do the hiring process tomorrow, which will give us two 'employees' on sight immediately, leaving us a day or two at most for equipment installation and testing. Our research must tell us by tomorrow which options are technically doable," Nick said.

Scanning the room, seeing nods from all, del Mundo said, "OK, let's get at it." With a chorus of "Hoorah," the work ensued.

After the next morning's in-character walk, exercise, and a light breakfast, Nick called Corbone, who said the two new employees could come to his office for paperwork, uniforms, and credentials and then a walk-through to get acquainted with the building. They could come immediately to get started. Nick contacted del Mundo, who said Smith and Jones were ready and on the way. The next call was to the rabbi, whom Nick updated on the previous night's activity and direction. The rabbi agreed that security issues would be much less of an obstacle if they could complete the action pre-election. He reminded Nick that regardless of who occupied the White House, he would still be president / chairman of the committee. He was off to a meeting and told Nick to keep him up to speed.

"It is a busy morning, Mom. Did you enjoy seeing your friends last night?"

"Wowoof."

With Mom kibbled and munching a Milk-Bone, Nick's phone rang. "Hello, Mr. Hawkins, it's Gene Williams here."

"Hi, Gene, how are you doing?" asked Nick

"Busy and busier with the polls turning in our favor. Mr. Korsikov had an associate in the ranch area who looked at it and was impressed. He wondered if we could get together later."

"Today?"

"If possible. I know this is short notice, but you stressed the time considerations of your friend, so Mr. Korsikov is proceeding hastily."

"This is fast action, thanks. What time are you thinking?"

"Say four o'clock at the same meeting room if you can make it."

"I will see about changing my schedule. If you don't hear from me in the next thirty minutes, then I will see you at four."

"Good. I hope you can work it out."

"I'm pretty sure I can. See you later." To Mom he said, "It looks like you get to be invisible again this afternoon."

"Rruff."

The next call was del Mundo on the sat phone. "Hey, Nick, the crew worked most of last night, and after Smith and Jones left, Black continued. The systems we are looking at will be completely adaptable for our purpose. Black has ordered some components and is in the shop building others. The delivery is scheduled for late afternoon, and he will be finished with his fabrications this evening. Working tonight, everything should be completed and synchronized, ready for installation."

"That is good. I spoke with the rabbi, and he agrees that an after-election encounter would be more complicated in terms of security and scrutiny. The crew's fast progress has us still within our preferred time frame. Do we have enough material in the can for the encounter to be convincing?"

"This agenda has been so blatant and the candidate's actions so flagrant that we will have time for only a fraction of the material. Don't forget, this is the longest-running twenty-four-seven fake reality-TV show in history."

"I wish this were forgettable, not even happening."

"We must do what we can now, especially since we are too late to change the election result. If we can make our plan work, then we can salvage a barely tolerable outcome from an otherwise catastrophic reality," del Mundo said.

"Yes," Nick said, "it will be very close, but if we offer only two options—one we prefer, the other we can deal with—then we have a good chance of thwarting the package agenda's long-term goal in either case."

"Talk to you later. Keep the faith."

"Roger, out."

In character, Nick and Mom took a slow walk to the tower and found a busy lobby again. Arriving five minutes early to the meeting room, Nick was welcomed by Williams. Mom evidently was permanently invisible.

"Hello, Mr. Hawkins. Glad you could make it. Coffee?"

"Yes, thank you."

Korsikov and a younger man joined them a few minutes later. Shaking hands, Korsikov said, "Good to see you. May I present my assistant, Igor. Igor, Mr. Hawkins."

They shook hands all around and then sat. Korsikov began: "Our associate was in the area and looked at the ranch. He was very impressed, said he thought the declared value of the property was accurate or possibly understated. He is familiar with the area and of properties in this value range and believes this project offers high earning potential. We have discussed the offering with the candidate, who is also impressed. We have a preliminary plan that has his real-estate company making the purchase with funding assistance provided by our bank. Transactions of this magnitude can be complicated, but having completed several large real estate purchases recently, we see no stumbling blocks. We are in a proceed mode, and our pieces are in place, but we must realize that even cash sales require a certain amount of time to complete. Our question is whether a closing by the end of the year will be timely enough for your friend's situational constraints."

"I am glad that I haven't wasted your time with my friend's situation. I will talk to him and describe your interest and ask if this time line will be satisfactory," Nick said. "After I talk to him, should I call Mr. Williams?"

Korsikov gave him a card and said Williams was getting busier with the campaign and he should call him directly.

"Good, then. I should be able to reach him this evening so will probably call you tomorrow."

"That will be fine," Korsikov said as he stood up. "I don't mean to be brusque, but I have more meetings so must go. I await your call."

"OK, until tomorrow."

With Igor mumbling a "Nice to meet you," the Russians left.

"To me, this sounded crazy with such huge amounts of money, and I felt guilty about mentioning a friend's problem."

"Not to worry, Mr. Hawkins. It seems that your bringing it up was a good thing," Williams said.

"Yes, it's funny how things work out sometimes. Thank you again for the call, and I'll see you later."

"Yes, you have a good evening," Williams said as they shook hands. Nick and his invisible boss took a slower, more rambling walk than usual. They spotted no followers and were home just before dark.

Checking in with del Mundo, Nick learned that Smith and Jones were now employees, with uniforms and ID badges and had surveyed the building and systems. They could foresee no problems and were working with Black to finish constructing the devices they would need. The component delivery had arrived, and all pieces were fitting together as planned. They would have both audio and video of the candidate's quarters, and one elevator would be fitted with a replacement mirror panel that was also a monitor, which would be easily changed out, leaving no tracks. The micro-cameras that the drones fitted in the air duct grills would be treated with a phosphorous coating that, when activated with a certain frequency, would melt, leaving only a small drop that would be taken for a weld spot. The metal ducting would be connected to an audio pickup, turning the system into a large microphone sending sound waves to their computer, which would translate and record everything. The hardware assembly should be completed and tested, ready for installation by morning. They would have a time window before the vote to accomplish their task.

"Good work by the crew," Nick told del Mundo. "We have a chance to do this before everything gets crazy."

"Yes, and after the encounter, the computers can be quickly packed, secured, and removed from the building unseen. The only evidence left will be the micro-cameras, which can be remotely melted at any time. The mirror monitor will be replaced and speakers removed following the encounter, and the malfunction will be attributed to one or more faulty relays, which the maintenance crew will find." Del Mundo's play-by-play made the tricky maneuvers sound simple.

"The only question now is timing, and I may have the solution for that," Nick said. "If we can have all our goodies installed and tested by tomorrow, then the window will be open. The unknown at this point is when the candidate will be alone on that elevator. We are working a sting, and I will have a meeting downstairs with the Russian banker who is to finance a real estate purchase for the candidate's company. I will request a short meet with the candidate at the next meeting, just ask if he could drop in for minute to say hi to a PAC donor and maybe sign an autograph. His bodyguards are always on call, waiting at the mezzanine-level Starbucks, where he picks them up for the escalator ride to the ground floor. We will have the modified elevator on hold and send it for him when he is leaving the penthouse. On the way down, it will stall between floors and the encounter will happen. If he picks up his guards and continues to the meeting then I will get a close-up look at how he is reacting. If he does not show up after the encounter, then that will tell us something. Either way, when he exits the elevator, our remote control will send it for the equipment removal and crew service, which discovers the faulty relays, makes replacements, and files the report. The possibility of him discussing the event with anyone is extremely low, especially with no evidence left behind. We will still have audio-video feeds from the residence and be able to melt the only remaining pieces if needed."

"That was a mouthful," del Mundo said. "Let's make sure the installations are ready tomorrow, and then you can set your meeting."

"Sounds good. Talk to you tomorrow." Nick signed off.

The morning was overcast as Nick and Mom took the in-character walk, exercised in the park, and went home to the sweep, kitchen sounds, and Milk-Bone.

"Can you handle French toast with bacon and fruit this morning?" Helen asked.

"Just what I had in mind."

"I get nervous when you are so agreeable."

"Nervous is good for you," said Nick, risking abuse.

"We can deal with your inane statements later. Sit down."

Doing as he was told, Nick enjoyed his breakfast as Mom happily crunched her kibble.

The sat phone squawked, and del Mundo was speaking. "The uniforms fit. Smith and Jones surveyed the building and found no unforeseen challenges. Black worked most of the night, and all three worked early this morning, have finished the equipment build, and will install first thing. The fitting and testing should have us online and ready by lunchtime. The temporary employees did not raise any eyebrows. They were as invisible as your boss. They will alert us when we are green light."

"Good. When they confirm our ready status and the candidate presence and schedule, I will ask to meet with Williams and the banker and request a minute to meet the candidate and have an autograph for the PAC members at home," Nick said.

"Good. Talk to you soon."

Dialing the rabbi, Nick wondered if getting too late a start to prevent the election result would render their plan a last-ditch effort with little impact. Voicing this concern with the rabbi brought a strong response. "The 'October surprise' changed the trajectory, and we will need time to delve into what influences prompted the FBI director's statements. Whether this was part of the Russian influence or not will be determined in time, just not right now. Our plan gives us two options, one of which the candidate will take. Either direction has consequences that can be used to protect our democracy. His choice will be about a lesser of evils. Remember, we have a powerful ace in the hole that provides intel and a strong deterrence capability. This card will be played in only the direst circumstance and could remain undetected indefinitely.

Our intel shows no candidate trips scheduled outside the tower until the vote, so we have a reasonable window for our action. Keep the faith, and keep me advised."

"That was reassuring, a regular pump up."

"Wowoof."

Nick spent time studying his notes while Mom rested, one eye watching her partner.

He called Corbone, who assured him that his two regular employees were very happy with their paid free time with bonuses and that Smith and Jones were not even noticed—just anonymous maintenance crew. No ripples yet. Nick thanked him and then took the call from del Mundo.

"The equipment is in place, tested, and fully operational. The candidate is watching cable news and busily tweeting. His schedule calls for scattered phone calls and staff meetings for the next three days with still no outside activities. We are ready for your schedule."

"Good. I will make contact and arrange the banker meeting and request the quick candidate meet and autograph."

"We are standing by, locked and loaded, poised and ready for your call."

"Roger." He turned to Mom. "Well, Mom, we are on ready status. It could be show-time today."

"Rruff."

The next call was to Korsikov, who answered after two rings. "Good morning, Mr. Korsikov. I was able to reach my friend at the ranch last night. He thinks your closing schedule could be workable but has some questions. Would we be able to get together this afternoon?"

"Yes, good, we could meet, but it would have to be later as my schedule is packed. Would five o'clock be OK for you?"

"Let me look. Yes, that would be fine. Do you think the candidate could spare a minute to meet a donor, and would it be too much to ask for an autograph for the PAC back home?"

"That sounds reasonable. Let me check with the campaign and get back to you."

"Thank you. I realize this request may sound trivial, but sometimes a small gesture can have a big impact."

"Yes, that is true, and this sounds to me like an unimposing request. I will confirm with you soon."

"Here we go again with a baited hook in the water."

"Woof."

In the kitchen at lunchtime, Helen said, "I hope you will like a tuna melt with tomato soup."

"I could not be happier with this menu. Your culinary skills are outstanding, which makes me wonder about other skills you may have."

"You would be very surprised."

Nick was unsure where this could lead. Although Helen was very attractive, she worked hard to conceal her beauty with a drab housekeeper appearance. *Easy boy, business first. Don't be distracted,* he thought. Lunch was nourishing and tasty, as was Mom's kibble allowance.

The next incoming call was from Williams. "Mr. Korsikov is tied up and wanted me to call you. The candidate is in the tower and would be happy to look in on the meeting later to say hello and give you a short, signed note for your PAC. He did want you to know that although he can spare only a few minutes, this short time is only due to his schedule, not to be taken as a sign of the PAC being viewed as a minor entity. He will arrange more time for you at a later date and apologizes for the brevity his schedule dictates."

"That is very kind of him, and the guys back home will be thrilled. Hopefully, we will see you also."

"Of course. I will see you at five; wouldn't miss it," Williams said.

The next call was to del Mundo. "Hey, Professor, it's show-time. I am meeting the banker at five o'clock today, and the candidate has agreed to drop by for a short meet and to give me an autograph to take home to the PAC. Are we ready?"

"Yes, the equipment is tested, up and running, all systems go. The rabbi is working on the encounter video, which will be completed within the hour and then messengered to the maintenance office, secreted within a carton of cleaning supplies. You will have to keep the meeting going until he gets into the elevator, at which point your phone will vibrate our code. If he is too shaken from the elevator experience to make an appearance at your meeting, then we will vibrate the phone with that code, and you can finish up and get out of the building. If he shows, then you will get a good read of his demeanor. After he leaves, get out of the building."

"Got it. I don't know which result is preferable."

"We won't know that until later. The crew will clean up the elevator as planned but will still have remotely controlled eyes and ears on his quarters. His immediate reactions will be informative. Good luck."

"Thanks," Nick said to a broken connection. "OK, Mom, game on."

"Wowoof."

With a last-minute call to del Mundo reconfirming all-systems readiness, they took the slow walk to the tower, approaching from the opposite direction from home.

The lobby was busy again, and Williams greeted them at the meeting room. "Hello, Mr. Hawkins. We are a bit early, and Mr. Korsikov will be right along."

"Good to see you, Gene," Nick said. "I'll just sit down if that is OK."

"Of course. Help yourself to coffee if you like."

"That is a good idea. I haven't had my nap so could use a little jolt." He sat down with his coffee at the table where Mom was already lying, invisible as usual.

Soon afterward, Korsikov bustled in, carrying a thick folder of papers. "Good afternoon, Mr. Hawkins. Good to see you so soon. I was not sure how quickly you would be able to reach your friend."

"The ranch situation is a priority for him, so he is very responsive to my calls. Provided there is an acceptable offer, he thinks the end of the year would be pushing it but would work. He wonders whether payment would be in the form of a cashier's check or wire transfer."

"The funding could be done either way he prefers. Due to his urgency, we have decided to forgo our normal negotiating strategy of starting with a very low offer and working from there. Instead, we will offer $210 million, which we feel is fair, maybe slightly low but having to act quickly, still fair."

"Of course, this is not my decision," Nick told him, "but to a simple farmer, this is an unimaginable amount of money. I would be very surprised if this is not acceptable, and I am comfortable presenting this offer, which will produce a fast response."

"Very good. I have brought you the paperwork documenting the offer and terms."

"I will send the paperwork next-day delivery so his attorney can get started. Again, not my decision, but my guess is that you will have yourselves a ranch." Nick's phone vibrated with the "go" code, so he continued. "Gene, do I still get to meet the candidate and get an autograph to take back to the PAC?"

"Yes, definitely. We are very grateful for your support, and he will be here shortly."

Upstairs, the candidate got into the elevator, in a hurry to get this insignificant chore over with. He hit the button for the mezzanine, where he would pick up his security man. The door closed, and the car descended rapidly and then came to a stop between floors. Cursing, he pushed buttons to no avail. Next, an altered voice began as the wall mirror lit up with images.

"Watch and listen closely," the voice intoned as the screen showed a long-forgotten scene of the candidate cavorting with two naked women in a hotel room of Russian decor. The party scene quickly shifted to a meeting with the Russian security chief and the candidate discussing cyber techniques and media manipulation to sway the election. The scene then changed to a series of the candidate's meetings with autocratic rulers and oligarchs making business deals for his company in the United States and abroad. Next was a discussion with the Russian president telling him that his dealings could be revealed or the cyber and other Russian involvement could guarantee his election. Following Moscow's instructions going forward would ensure the tapes would never be released, and he could be the president.

The voice continued, "We are a small group of patriots who have been active since the Civil War. What you have seen is only a fraction of what we have. You made your choice of the Russian options; now you must choose from our options. The Russian strategies are very effective, and in days you will be declared the president-elect.

One option for you is to disregard us and continue with the charade, in which case we will immediately release enough damaging evidence to prevent you from ever taking office and have you facing charges that could include conspiracy, collusion with a foreign power, and possibly even treason. You will be politically and personally ruined and probably imprisoned. We will also paint you as a double agent witness working against Moscow. Their zeal in eliminating any witness against them has been documented many times over many years. Your other option is to continue as you are, seemingly following Moscow's direction while secretly sharing information with us and following our orders. We would then not publish any material and would let you serve as president for one term only. We view the Russians as an even larger threat than you, and your assistance in bringing them to justice will earn our protection. Your choice is simple. You may live with us or die without us. Do not take us lightly. You have no idea what we are capable of. You have twenty-four hours to make your choice and either call the number on the screen or not. Know also that if you discuss this event with anyone, we will know and assume your choice to be without us. Have a nice day."

There was silence. The screen became a mirror again, and the elevator continued its descent.

The candidate got out at the mezzanine shakily and found his bodyguard. The elevator door closed, and the car headed up. He wanted nothing more than to retreat to his gilded lair but was afraid to attract attention by skipping a minor meeting with a PAC. With his body-guard, he rode the escalator to the lobby and entered the meeting room. He made a hasty greeting, gave Nick a thank-you note with his signature, and begged off, citing his overloaded schedule. With his bodyguard, he got into a different elevator and headed to his penthouse, feeling sick to his stomach.

Meanwhile, the modified elevator was routed to the basement service area, where Smith and Jones removed their equipment and left two worn-out relays with a repair report on Corbone's desk. They then got into the van waiting in the garage and left the building. They changed from the uniforms on the ride to the dock, where another crew member drove the van away as they got into the waiting launch to the *Bubble*.

"That was quick, but I'm real glad I got to meet the candidate," Nick told Williams. "He seemed a little under the weather. I hope he is OK."

"I'm sure he is fine. Just been going nonstop for weeks so is probably a bit run down."

"I hope you are right. Mr. Korsikov. I expect to hear from my friend quickly and will contact you the minute I do."

"Thank you. I shall look forward to hearing from you," Korsikov said. "I must get to my next meeting now. Maybe with a positive response from your friend, we will be able to have lunch or dinner at our next get-together."

"That would be nice. Take care," Nick told him. "Gene, I am running out of steam and must be getting along myself. Thanks again."

"Yes, Mr. Hawkins, you take care also," Williams said as Nick and the still-invisible Mom slowly walked out.

Back in the safe house, after a tender rib eye with baked potato, artichoke, and fresh-baked dinner rolls, Nick allowed himself a glass of good Silver Oak Cabernet. Helen joined him, and Mom joined her kibble.

Later, in black night gear, Nick and Mom took the shadow route to the dock, hopped onto the launch, and joined the crew on the *Bubble*.

"Good job, everyone," del Mundo announced. "Watching the video encounter was very entertaining. The candidate was shocked, to put it mildly, and must have left a sweat puddle on the floor. How was he at your meeting, Nick?"

"He was white as a ghost, sweating visibly, and couldn't wait to get out of there."

Del Mundo summarized: "We have left the micro-cameras, which can be destroyed remotely, if necessary, and the ducting still provides audio and is operated remotely with the transmitters and relays built into the metalwork, undetectable. The elevator is normal, with the repair report and worn-out relays in the file. He did send one security man to check out the car, but there was nothing to be found. A mystery. We are still unknown and most likely will remain so. No tracks."

"Don't forget that we still have the ranch sting in motion, so it will be interesting to see how this plays out," Nick said.

"He might think this is a real deal and that he can pull it off. If we let him close the purchase, we will be much closer, maybe close enough to wrap up the Russians," del Mundo said.

Nick texted a "mission accomplished" to the rabbi's phone, which soon did the clicks and buzzes. The rabbi was speaking, and Nick put it on speaker. "Nice work, everybody. If that went pretty much according to plan and regardless of how he chooses, then we have recourse. Remember also that we have a powerful ace in the hole as an emergency defense of our democracy."

"Which choice do you think he will make?" Nick asked.

"That is hard to predict. This is not a normal, rational person. Time will tell. Stay tuned."

Chapter 12

●　　●　　●

CLEAN UP, TECH CHECK, SET THE STING SCHEDULE

The next day, after Nick and Mom had their morning exercise and basic breakfast of bacon and eggs for Nick and kibble for Mom, Nick checked in with Corbone.

"Good morning, Mr. Corbone. This is Neil Miller. How are your elevators running?"

"Oh, hello, good morning to you. Everything seems to be working just fine. We had a short visit from a campaign security man who did a cursory inspection and found no problems with the cars. I showed him the service report, and he seemed satisfied. Your workers are still registered with our company as temporary help, so they could be activated if needed. Just let me know. The regulars enjoyed their time off."

"Thank you," Nick said. "That may be a possibility. Please contact me if you have any further scrutiny or questions."

"Roger, will do. Thanks again for helping my family."

"You're welcome, and thank you. Talk to you later." After hanging up, he said, "Well, Mom, the ruse is holding up so far."

"Rroof."

The next call was to the rabbi, who was watching the clock as the candidate's twenty-four-hour response deadline approached.

"Do you think he will make the call?" Nick asked.

"I think he will make this first call, even if as a stall to buy time as he settles down. He did seem genuinely shaken by the elevator incident."

"He appeared very nervous and just popped in and out of our meeting. He did not really look well."

"Adding to his stress is the difficulty of him talking about it. This story will just sound crazy and will have the people around him questioning his mental state. Add in our threats if he does say anything, and I will be surprised if he does not make the call before the deadline. Whether he will fall into line or just stall and continue pushing the agenda is another matter. He is running a race to grab enough power to squash any challenges before the committee can stop him. We know he has Congress cowed down and is delegitimizing the media constantly. He will certainly create many false claims to distract the intelligence agencies and sidetrack any bipartisan investigations. Don't forget that he will be able to fill a Supreme Court seat with a supporter. Add it all up, and we have a close race. We have a few hours on the clock, so we will soon know how he plays this. We will talk after the deadline or sooner if he calls early. Either way, the ranch deal will be a part of the action."

Nick's phone rang with del Mundo on the line. "We have been monitoring our boy all morning. Our mini-cameras are there, and the audio is still functional with some fading in and out as he changes rooms. He is still visibly upset, moving about, watching cable news, and keeping to himself. He has taken only a couple of calls, one from Korsikov. They spoke of the ranch deal and were enamored about the fast, large profit they expected. They agreed that their end would be lucrative while helping their 'aluminum king' friend along the way. There has been no mention at all about the elevator show. The rabbi obviously got his attention, and he doesn't seem to have decided how to play this. I think the fact that he is so far keeping the secret means a good chance that he will not ignore the deadline and will make the call. He will make that move regardless of whether he plays ball or not."

"We are all in accord on that. Corbone reports only a quick check of the elevators by candidate's security, which we knew about, so for now that trail is not being followed. Our temporary employees are still registered and can be put back to work if needed."

"If he does make the call, then we will need to get together to plan our next move, which will obviously include the ranch deal," del Mundo said. "If he does not call or calls and then stalls, we will need to take action to either bring him around or to take him down quickly. Let's plan on meeting here on the *Bubble* before the deadline so we are ready either way."

"Good plan. See you in a while." He said to Mom, "Let's see if Helen can find us some lunch."

"Woof."

Soon it was near deadline, and Nick and Mom, in costume, took a walk. After cab rides and changes of direction, they were picked up at a commercial pier by the launch for the short ride to the *Bubble*. With greetings and rubs from Smith and Black, Mom was beaming.

"Thanks for bringing your boss," said Smith.

"Rroof."

On the *Bubble,* del Mundo met them in the dining/conference room, which had audio and video tuned in to the penthouse. The audio feed was good, and the video feed from the living area was live but showed only empty rooms.

"He has been holed up in his bedroom suite all day, so not much video, but our audio is picking up everything. If the call happens, we will be able to hear both sides. The rabbi knows we are online and listening, ready to plan the next move based on the call or no call. We are closing in on the last hour."

With the entire team—Smith, Jones, Black, del Mundo, Merrit, Nick, and Mom—waiting expectantly, the tension mounted.

"We are in the final hour," del Mundo said. "Better buckle our seat belts."

After a few minutes, the candidate came into view of the office minicamera and sat at his desk, looking rumpled and fidgety. He picked up the phone and dialed. They heard clicks and buzzes and then the rabbi's altered voice.

"Hello. I am glad you made the smart decision to make this call. Understand that we would rather you be viewed as a patriot than a traitor. By working with us to protect our democracy, you will be able to serve one term and leave office with a good reputation and no adverse legal consequences. You will need only to follow our directives to protect our national security. The evidence you were shown is but a fraction of material we have that proves many violations of various criminal statutes and would be devastating to you politically and personally. If you reject us, then we will begin the release and initiate criminal charges, which would include collusion with a foreign government, conflicts of interest, violations of the emolument clause, and possibly treason. As you have seen, we have conclusive proof to back up these allegations. On the other hand, if you do indeed work with us to counter the foreign attackers, none of the evidence against you will see the light of day. You will be elected and permitted to serve one term. Then you will return to your private life and business as a patriot, a strong president. We will protect you from any repercussions from your actions, which only we are capable of. Your call today is a good decision and will allow us to hold our actions for now, allowing your election and preparations for the inauguration. We will consult on a regular basis to guide you through your actions as president. Again, by following our directions, you will be permitted one term in office, after which you will step down with respect, no charges filed or secrets revealed. Do you understand and agree to these terms?"

"Yes, I see what you are saying, and I get the point."

"Does that mean that you agree to these terms?"

"Yes, it is the only acceptable option, so I am in."

"Thank you. You have made a wise decision. There will be times when following our instructions is difficult, but not as difficult as not doing so. Some actions may seem illogical and not make sense to you, but they will be important to our overall strategy and must be taken. We will use this phone system for now but could change to a different system in the future. Congratulations on a wise decision. Enjoy your coming victory, and don't let yourself, your family, and the rest of us down. We will be back in contact soon." Click and done.

In the tower, the candidate appeared tired or resigned, slumped in his gold-plated chair for a bit, and then moved back to his suite, out of camera sight. The audio equipment picked up sounds of cursing and stomping around.

The team on the *Bubble* didn't know whether to cheer or not after listening to the call. Del Mundo said he thought the cursing and stomping indicated frustration at being forced to comply with the terms as laid out by the rabbi and reasoned that if the candidate planned to ignore the instructions, he wouldn't appear so angry.

Nick said, "This guy is a compulsive liar, so regardless of his stated agreement with conditions, why believe him? He just recognized the need to buy time for now and will only pay lip service for as long as it takes to consolidate control over all branches of government, at which point he will thumb his nose at any instructions. With the total control he is working toward, he believes he will be untouchable, which could be the case."

Nick's phone on speaker rang, followed by the clicks and buzzes, and the rabbi was speaking. "I assume we all heard the call, narrowly meeting the deadline. I have mixed feelings about his sincerity and am certain only that the call was to buy him time, avoiding our taking action immediately. We anticipated this, so after he wins the election in the next few days, the real test will begin. After being elected, legitimately or not, he will have more to lose, ramping up the pressure. Our consensus on the committee is that he will appear to go along with our directives provided we don't order him to make any overtly hostile moves against his Russian backers. This will also allow us more time to develop our strategy and enact the ranch sting to ensnare Russian players. When that trap is sprung, the environment will change dramatically with our planned surprise. That is when the candidate will reveal his real choice. For now, we let him have more rope to fashion a tighter noose. I must go now. Please advise me of anything notable from the tower, and let's talk later."

"I agree with the rabbi and the committee. He will be elected and have more to lose, which will have him acting like he is cooperating," del Mundo said.

"Yes," Nick said, "our focus now should be on the ranch deal, which has the possibility of snaring a Russian money-man and exposing the pay-to-play activities of the candidate. After the election results, which we already know, we should allow a day of celebration while pressing this purchase forward. It is the owner's need to sell quickly for personal reasons, so our haste is to be expected. I will begin planning the details of this adventure so we can move right away."

They all nodded in accord, and Nick and Mom were soon on the launch, disembarking at a different dock, and headed home to work on the ranch schedule.

Tuesday brought the expected results, thanks to the powerful combination of hacking, massive media manipulation, and the FBI director's announcement of a new investigation of the Democratic candidate—the "October surprise."

After breakfast and the morning walk, the sweep, and kitchen sounds from Helen, they tucked into the French toast and bacon, fruit, and coffee. Mom was happily crunching her kibble as Nick called Williams to offer congratulations. "Hey, Gene, we really did it. Congrats, good job."

"Yes, it seemed such a long shot, but we actually pulled it off."

"Now we can really get the country moving again," Nick said, laying it on.

"You're right. The candidate has a big something to crow about, and he should."

"Please pass on the congratulations from our little PAC. I will be by there soon to meet with Korsikov and will see you then."

"OK, and I will pass along your message."

"Thanks. See you soon."

The next call to Korsikov involved some mutual back-slapping and a lunch date the following day at the grill in the tower. "It will be a madhouse, but we can use a private dining room where we will be able to hear ourselves think and talk. Will one o'clock be good for you?" Korsikov asked.

"That will be fine. I think you will be pleased with my friend's response," Nick said.

As he was about to call the rabbi, Nick's phone rang. "Hi, Neil," Corbone said. "I know you are probably busy with everything going on, but we may have a problem. There was a complaint from a tenant about the elevator problem, and the tenant wants one of his people to delve into the incident, ostensibly from fear that a further glitch could be harmful. This sounded far-fetched, and

I tried to downplay the incident and any safety concerns, but he was adamant about having his people check out everything."

"You were right to call me. Do we have a schedule when his man will do this inspection?"

"Yes. I set the inspection for tomorrow evening at six o'clock, when the building traffic should be tapering off."

"Did he say who he was sending?"

"Only that he was a security consultant, an engineer named Boris."

"Great, another Russian. I don't like the sound of a Russian security operative digging too deeply, certain to have questions about our service workers. That would be too close for both of us."

"What should I do?" Corbone asked.

"Just go through your regular routine. Let your crew leave on time so they are out of the way. This little party will probably require extreme action on our part to remove the threat. Don't worry. We are used to this type of situation and will keep you out of harm's way, making sure you are not implicated in the problems this man will have."

"That sounds good except for having to miss all the excitement."

"I am sorry about that, but it is important that you know nothing, see nothing, and can play dumb later—especially because the action will happen right outside your office door. At the time of the action, you will need to be on a regular call or e-mail that can backstop your story of a technician not showing up for an appointment. And there can be no live video feeds from the hallway, so some splicing afterward will be necessary. One of our temps will be on hand to manage that chore."

"You sure came up with a solution at the spur of the moment," Corbone said.

This situation reminded Nick of missions in the Middle East, where rescuing hostages or removing double agents required thinking on his feet for his survival and the survival of others. His extensive training and combat experience allowed him to succeed, even when he seemingly had no chance.

"That is just what we do," he told Corbone. "I will be there at five o'clock to make any final preparations or changes as necessary. Don't worry; this will be a simple operation, and we will be prepared for Boris, even if he shows up with an assistant."

"OK, I'll see you then," Corbone said and hung up.

Now, back to the rabbi call.

"Hey, Nick, what's up?"

"Lots. I am meeting Korsikov tomorrow for lunch. I will tell him that my friend thinks the offer is low but, considering his circumstances and time constraints, will accept. His only condition is that all parties meet at the ranch for the closing. That will be explained by his inability to travel and insistence that he meet the buyers on-site in person as his Midwestern honesty dictates. Presented in this manner, the reaction will be more pity than suspicion. The more concerning part of tomorrow's schedule happens at six o'clock in the evening when Corbone is scheduled to have a security engineer from the campaign tenant arrive to look into the elevator incident. I will need a van and two large crates in the underground garage with the usual removable plumbing-company signs. The checker is a Russian, Boris. The van needs to be in place by five o'clock, and the two crates are in case he brings an assistant. I will also need Smith with me for technical details and backup in case of an assistant. Corbone will be in his office on phone calls when everything happens, so he will know only that the guy was a no-show. This should go smoothly, and we will need to keep Boris on ice for only a few weeks or deported if possible. Other than these chores, it should be an easy day."

"It sounds like you will be a little busy. The logistics on my end are no problem. Do we need some forgetful-med kits?"

"Yes, the whole kits would be a good idea."

"OK, done. Keep me posted."

Checking the picture/bio file from the rabbi, he found one Boris, who might be the inspector. This one had an engineering background as well as security history and a list of dropped charges of strong-arm assaults. If this was that Boris, then all the precautions were important, and Nick knew he would have to be on his game while dealing with this dangerous operative. After hours of gaming the next day's activities, with energy bars and water for lunch, Nick was hungry and asked Helen if there was anything for dinner. Mom heard the mention of dinner and gave a little "Wowoof" to let him know that she, too, was interested in eating.

Fed and watered, they were back upstairs for more planning. Nick called del Mundo. "Hi, Professor. I have a lunch meet with Korsikov tomorrow that will be simple. Later, I have a chore that will not be so simple, and I will need Smith on hand." After Nick outlined what he had in mind, del Mundo thought it workable and said Smith would be good.

With more planning and gaming possibilities, Nick fell asleep late. Morning brought the exercise walk in costume, then their return back home. After the sweep and kitchen sounds, Helen announced a big eggs Benedict breakfast for Nick's "needed strength" for the day. The hollandaise sauce was as good as the previous one, and Nick expressed his gratitude. Mom did the same with her kibble soaked with the bacon drippings.

After more studying and calls to Corbone and del Mundo, Nick and Mom, in costume, headed to the tower with a leisurely roundabout walk. The lobby was the busiest Nick had seen it—groups of supporters packed into all corners, loudly celebrating the election. Bumped and jostled, they made their way to the private dining room. Williams was the only person in the room, and he greeted Nick happily.

"We did it, Mr. Hawkins, even though no one said we had a chance. We could have never pulled it off without the generous support of groups like yours," he said with enthusiasm as he shook Nick's hand.

"Right, Gene. Now we can get the country moving in the right direction."

"Yes. The president-elect asked me to sit in for him today with you. He has events stacked up all day but wants me to assure you that he is very excited about this deal."

"That is understandable. Please convey my congratulations again when you see him," Nick said.

"Will do, Mr. Hawkins, and here is Mr. Korsikov."

Korsikov entered, shook hands, and sat. The portly Russian was dressed in a navy-blue suit, white shirt, and striped tie. The suit was outdated like Nick's—boxy and ill-fitting in the Russian bureaucratic style. "Good day, Mr. Hawkins. Nice to see you—that is, if you bring good news."

"Good seeing you also, Mr. Korsikov, and yes, I believe you will find the news positive."

"Excellent. Let's have lunch, and then we can discuss things with full bellies."

"You are a man speaking wisely. What do you recommend?"

"The chef has prepared Kobe beef grilled steak sandwiches with French fries and a special coleslaw, if that would suit your palate."

"I could not have chosen better," Nick said.

The lunch was excellent, and the crafty Mom demonstrated great control by remaining silent and invisible while the rich beef aroma had her nose twitching. After they were sated, Nick began. "My friend thinks the offer is low, but the time constraints he is facing and your ability to act quickly will have the offer acceptable, with one condition. Being a somewhat old-fashioned rancher, he will be comfortable if the deal is closed with all parties at the ranch for the transaction. He has always done business personally and hopes we can appreciate his need to look the people that he is dealing with in the eye. He also has pride in this property he built and wants to feel good about selling to you and know that you can see and appreciate in person what you are buying. He hopes that this request is acceptable and appreciates your humoring him. Selling the ranch is difficult for him, so respecting his comfort level will have everything go easier."

"I don't find this condition unreasonable. I might have requested it myself, as I have learned to always personally see what I am investing in. He may rest assured that we will be delighted to have our closing meeting on-site, and maybe his chef can provide an exotic meal of some kind," Korsikov said.

"Good. I am sure his chef can amaze us. We now must set a date for the closing. My sense is that sooner is better for all parties. My friend is at or near the ranch and has no travel plans, so he is available at your earliest convenience."

"I too have no travel plans for the near term and would also like to complete the transaction quickly. I will speak with the president-elect and see how quickly he can spare an afternoon. He knows this must be done as soon as possible and will likely schedule this short trip very soon. I will be with him later and in the morning, so we should have a schedule by tomorrow afternoon."

"That will be good. Thank you for an enjoyable lunch, and I look forward to hearing from you tomorrow," Nick said.

"It was my pleasure, and I am glad that you enjoyed it. I must go now and will call you tomorrow," Korsikov said before he left.

Nick said to Williams, "Gene, you were pretty quiet today. Are you OK?"

"Yes, I just figured you two had business that I am not involved in, so I stayed out of the discussion."

"Well, that's good, and maybe you can tell the president-elect to hurry a little."

"I probably don't need to say anything because he is already anxious to get this done," Williams said.

"Yes, you are probably right. There is a sizable potential profit involved. Thanks again, Gene. I must get going now. See you soon."

"Very good, Mr. Hawkins, take care."

Nick and the always-invisible Mom walked slowly with several stops, the cab shuffle, and the last three blocks on foot. After the sweep, the Helen sounds, and the

Milk-Bone, Nick dialed the rabbi. Clicks and buzzes, and then the rabbi was speaking. "How was lunch?"

"It was delicious, and Korsikov was happy with closing at the ranch and will talk with the president-elect to set a schedule as soon as possible. The greed will not allow them to delay. He said he'd call tomorrow with their schedule. On the other issue, tonight is the Russian checking the elevators, he thinks. We have guaranteed Corbone cover from blowback, and making good on that serves all our interests. I will need Smith to drive the van and meet Mom and me in the parking garage near the park, where we can be picked up out of sight. We have been seen leaving the building and will be unobserved in the van. It will park in the basement level, where the best space will be blocked off with a no-parking-service sawhorse. The cameras covering that area will be inoperable, and then a video feed showing nothing will be spliced into the loop when we are finished and gone. We will be waiting and pull a basic snatch of the Russian or Russians, pack into the van, and be gone. Simple is good."

"I get it. The snatch will be the only danger point, but you are used to that. We will keep them on ice, rotating them to different locations, and possibly find a reason to deport them, with no memory of what happened. Smith and the van will pick you up at the garage. Good luck."

"Roger that. Talk to you after."

With everything set, Nick had a rest and packed all the night op gear, and then he and Mom headed to the park. Moving slowly as usual, they found Smith with the van. "Hey, Smith, how are you doing?"

"Hi, Nick. Hi, Mom. It is good you brought your boss," Smith told him as Mom wiggled and woofed.

"Yeah, she likes to keep an eye on me."

"Lucky for you."

"You've got that right."

"Rrwoof."

Changing into the night gear as they rode, Nick checked with Corbone, who reported all in readiness with the hall and garage cameras on pause.

Nick suspected that the Russian would arrive early to put Corbone off balance, so he wanted to be in position to keep the action in the hall, leaving Corbone undisturbed in his office. He and Mom would wait in a maintenance closet down the hall from the office, watching a monitor feed from a mini-camera that Smith would install and check before waiting in the van, ready to move if Nick saw two people. Nick put on a maintenance jacket and cap, a glue-on beard, and semi-dark glasses so he could approach the quarry without alarm. Mom would wait in the closet, watching close and ready through the partially open door, while Nick pushed a cart toward the Russian.

Soon it was show-time with the Russian arriving early, as Nick had anticipated. As the Russian stepped out of the elevator, Nick saw that he was big: six and a half feet tall, thick, and muscled, with a shaved head and scarred face and a crooked nose, dressed in cargo pants, a shirt, and a windbreaker, under which the outline of a gun was visible. Nick knew this would not be easy.

The only good sign was that he had not brought an assistant, but he did not look anything like an easy mark. He walked down the hallway, and Nick, pushing the cart and looking down at his phone, veered toward the man. Looking up and putting the phone in his pocket, he acted surprised and straightened his path to leave room for the man to pass. Nick then faked a trip, turned the cart sharply to pin the man against the wall, said, "Excuse me," and acted as if he were moving the cart.

The Russian cursed and kicked the cart hard, knocking it over at Nick. Nick dove over the moving cart, going for a throat punch, which only partly connected. The Russian kicked again, catching Nick on the hip and creating some space while he pulled a silenced automatic from his waistband. Next was a roar and a black flash, and Mom had another Russian gun hand clamped in her jaws, and then there was a staccato rhythm of breaking bones and the gun rattling to the floor. Recovering from the kick, Nick tried to go over the cart with another punch, but the Russian kicked the cart again, knocking him off balance sending him tangled up with the cart and going down. Rolling and scrambling up, Nick saw a flash of steel, a knife, in the good hand of the Russian coming at him, stretching against Mom's hold on his other hand to reach him.

Nick barely avoided a slash to his face with Mom holding back the Russian. The Russian twisted back to go for Mom with the knife.

Nick yelled a command for Mom to release and back out, which she did, putting her out of reach of the knife hand crossing the brute's body. Then the knife was coming back around to Nick, who landed a stinging punch to the ear, which dazed the guy for a moment. Shaking his head to clear it, he brought the knife into play again but did not see Mom circling around behind him and was not prepared for the vise like clamp on his hand, breaking bones and making him drop the knife. As Mom pulled him off balance, Nick followed and landed a knee to the face with all his weight behind it, cracking the Russian's head on the floor.

He went limp: maybe out, maybe dazed, maybe playing possum. Nick briefly flashed back to a previous battle, wondering about the real condition of the man. He then got the needle in for the medication. Nick knew the fight was over, and his breathing slowed, his senses came back, and he reached for his partner. Hugging her, he told her what a good girl she was while Mom wiggled and woofed. "That guy was a load."

"Rruff."

Smith was there with the crate. He looked at the cargo and exclaimed, "What the hell is that?"

"A steroid-fueled giant with weapons," Nick said. "You can have the knife." They strapped the man into the crate with zip ties to the eyelets in the corners and trundled it to the van. Mom carried the dropped gun, and she and Nick cleaned up and changed to the Hawkins costumes while Smith retrieved the mini-camera and monitor and cleaned up the hall, removing all blood traces. He returned the cart and left the scene sterile and in its normal state.

Nick called Corbone, who said he had heard some crashes and bumps and asked Nick what had happened. Nick told him that his visitor had arrived early and was leaving early and that he could restore the hall video and the garage feed in five minutes. He asked Corbone to check the hall closet to make sure nothing was amiss before restarting the hallway video feed, and he would talk with him tomorrow.

With Nick securing the crate and then Mom happily crunching a Milk-Bone while Nick scratched her and told her what a good girl she was, Smith had them out of the building and into the rush hour traffic, just another contractor van among many, heading home from a hard day's work. Pulling into a different parking garage, Nick and Mom hopped out and took the slow, meandering walk home. After the sweep, Helen sounds, and a Milk-Bone for Mom, Nick asked Helen if there was a possibility for a light dinner. "How about a Caesar salad and smoked salmon, maybe a little ice-cold Chardonnay?"

"That will be perfect," he told her as he headed to the shower. "You are a very good girl," he told Mom from the shower. "I think you should have an extra Milk-Bone with your kibble tonight."

"Wowoof."

Nick finished cleaning up, dressed in cargos and T-shirt, and dialed the rabbi. He heard clicks and buzzes and then, "It's just a little after six. Are you OK? What happened?" The rabbi sounded apprehensive.

"Yes, fine, only a couple of bruises. Fortunately, there was only one—a trained giant who came close to getting off a shot after a kick knocked me back. Mom did her gun hand trick, which let me land a punch. The breaking bones and gun clattering to the floor sounded like a short drum solo. Then a knife drama, which Mom neutralized. This guy is over six and a half feet tall and probably close to three hundred pounds, a skilled brawler. He is all packed up, medicated, and ready for a vacation. I am having a light dinner, some Advil, and an ice pack, and checking out for the night. Mom will have extra Milk-Bones with her kibble and a nice rib-eye bone."

"It sounds like she saved your butt again."

"I could have handled it, but she saved me from some damage."

"I'm not sure why your boss puts up with you, but good work. And I just got word that Smith delivered the van and is back on board the *Bubble*. Our people will take it from here, and Smith will report to del Mundo. Have a nice sleep, and we will talk tomorrow."

Chapter 13

• • •

STING TIME, REPOSITION THE TEAM

Nick woke with a start but then relaxed as Mom's smiling face greeted his scratchy eye opening. Moving was a different thing, with bruises and strains making themselves known. "What?"

Mom cocked her head. "Rrrruf."

"You think I should get up and go for a walk, do you?"

"Ruff woof."

"OK, OK." And he was up and moving. With the in-costume welcome slow pace with rest stops, he was loosening up by the time they reached the park, glad he had no serious injuries. Mom had cleaned up well and showed no signs of yesterday's activities. Nick was looking for the logic of Mom doing the heavy lifting while he received the bruises, deciding only that her technique was superior to his. "You good girl."

"Rrrr."

His stretches were restricted but helped the tightness. The slow walk home was soothing, and he was feeling almost human when they arrived. Then with the sweep, Helen sounds, Milk-Bone for Mom, shower for him, it was kitchen time, home of the much-appreciated ice bag, which Nick applied as he sat at the table. To her credit, Helen kept a straight face, merely asking if a stack of pancakes, bacon, fruit, and coffee sounded good.

"That is just what I had in mind," Nick told her.

"That's good, because I just happen to have some batter all whipped up," she said with a sweet smile.

"Imagine that."

"Woof."

Ravenous, Nick stuffed himself. Then it was upstairs for the morning calls, Mom for her after-kibble nap.

Del Mundo called first. "Hey, Nick, how are you feeling? Smith said you had a little exercise last night."

"Just a light workout."

"It was probably a little lighter after your boss took the weapons out of play."

"Yeah, she likes to poke her nose into things."

"Oh yes, darn dog, she saved your butt again."

"She is the best."

Listening intently, Mom wiggled and stretched, groaning happily.

Del Mundo said, "Smith tells me this Russian was a dangerous giant and put up a fight, so we are all glad that you and Mom escaped serious injury. Now to business. I understand that you expect to have a schedule later today for the ranch deal. We can have the *Bubble* on anchor close to the ranch in less than a week's notice. This will have our technical capabilities within range, and Smith, Jones, and Black available for the site preparations and action. When the schedule is set, we can clear port here and proceed to the gulf."

"That will be helpful, and we will need to be at full strength to pull off this sting, which will be crucial to our finally getting in front of the agenda," Nick said. "The sooner we are on-site, the better; the preparations will be time consuming and must be installed and tested before the event. The timing involved will be critical for our strategy to be successful."

"If you could set the schedule with at least ten days' lead time, then we should have enough margin to make sure our systems are operational," del Mundo said.

"I will make sure we have at least that much of a window for operating," Nick said.

"Excellent. We will be ready to move when the date is firm. Talk to you later."

With that piece ready, Nick dialed the rabbi, and after the clicks and buzzes he was connected.

"Hi, Nick, how are you feeling?"

"Pretty good, thanks. I had a few sore spots this morning, but with a walk, breakfast, and shower, I am fine. The ice packs and ibuprofen are helping, and I am ready to go."

"You will be interested to know that your pal, Boris, has a long history of not being a very nice person. Multiple

charges of assault, including killings, have all been covered up and dismissed by the Russian government. As we
know, they like to protect their useful tools. He is now
being moved through several high-security installations
and interrogated. We can keep him off the radar for a few
weeks and then probably deport him. We will be interested in seeing who comes looking for him. If we move
quickly enough with the ranch deal, then his absence will
not impede our action."

"I expect to hear from Korsikov later to arrange the
schedule, which needs to be at least ten days out to give
del Mundo time to relocate the *Bubble,* which can be
anchored close enough to the ranch to be effective in
terms of logistics and electronics."

"Good. Please advise me when the date is set."

"Of course, and I will be checking with Corbone soon
to see if he has had any reaction to the no-show."

"Good. Talk to you soon. Give your boss an extra Milk-
Bone for me."

Mom, hearing herself talked about, was wiggling and
moaning.

"Yes, he thought you deserved an extra Milk-Bone, so
here."

"Wowoof," and then happy crunching.

Nick then called Corbone, who said he had not heard
from the tenant. "Was the scene cleaned up and restored,
video feeds fixed, everything made normal with no complications?" Nick asked.

"Yes, Mr. Miller. Everything is fine—no marks or stains or anything unusual with videos or anything else. I was on a logged phone call the entire time with a supplier, going over equipment lists and billings, so no problems here."

"Good work, thanks. I think it would be good if you called the tenant and reported the no-show of their man and ask if they would like to reschedule his appointment. The response will provide insight about their priorities and attitude. Can you make this call after lunch and then call me, and we can decide what steps to take to continue your protection?

Even after his huge breakfast, Nick was hungry again. Lunch was good, and he was back upstairs with fresh ice packs when Corbone rang. "Hey, Mr. Corbone, how was your call?"

"I had to bite my tongue to keep from laughing. The tenant seemed confused, not sure at first what I was talking about, and then recovered and said they would get back to me. I got the feeling that they were busy with higher-priority issues. I told them to let me know and that I would do whatever I could to help. He said thanks and hung up."

"Good work. It sounds like they are having trouble keeping up with a situation they are not prepared for, actually being elected, and may have no time for follow-ups. Please call if you have more questions, and thank you again."

"It is my pleasure, and I surely will call."

"It looks like our little adventure was effective," he told Mom.

"Woolf."

Still tired from the previous day's excitement, Nick got the ice bags and settled in for a nap, conking out quickly into a deep sleep, Mom curled up next to the bed, happy as always for a one-eye-open doze next to her partner.

After two hours that seemed like two minutes, he was awakened by the phone ringing.

"Good afternoon, Mr. Hawkins. Korsikov here. How are you?"

"Fine, thanks, just catching up on some reading. How are you doing?"

"Very well, thank you. The president-elect and I have just met and wondered if the Tuesday before Thanksgiving would be a good schedule for your friend. This would make getting away easier because of the holiday, which has him traveling that week anyway, and for me, anytime is good."

"Mr. Korsikov, when my friend said there was a timing issue, you folks took him seriously and are moving fast. I will contact him to confirm but am sure he will happy for your fast action. May I call you later?"

"Of course. When the date is set, we will make our flight plans. Looking at the brochure, we saw a landing strip and wondered if it could handle large jets."

"I can answer that as my friend is proud of the capabilities and has mentioned this on more than one occasion.

There is a small tower, manned on request, and a new large hangar with pilot lounge, and the runway has adequate length for a 747. Will you be flying anything larger than that?"

Laughing, Korsikov said, "No, not even close. This will make our travel much less time consuming and more convenient. We will be arriving from different directions in our own aircraft, so may we presume that the field can handle more than one aircraft?"

"Yes, that is no problem, and there are fuel trucks and maintenance facilities if needed."

"Good. I will await your call confirming the date, and we can discuss the timing then."

"OK, I will call after I reach my friend."

"I'll await your call."

A quick call to the ranch-owner friend confirmed what Nick already knew—that this schedule was good.

Next, he dialed the rabbi and, after the normal procedure, was connected. "I talked to Corbone, who had not been contacted, had him report the no-show to the tenant, and asked if they wanted to reschedule. They sounded busy to him and said they would call or not. Korsikov called with a date the Tuesday before Thanksgiving, which is fine with the ranch owner. This schedule will also give del Mundo time to relocate the *Bubble* in the gulf, close to the ranch, a short launch or rigid inflatable boat ride away. Korsikov also likes the landing strip and said he and the president-elect will be in separate aircraft, which will be conducive to our plans. I will finalize the date and alert del Mundo."

"Good. I will begin working on the plan now that we have a schedule." Click.

After delaying an hour, he called Korsikov. "I finally tracked down my friend, who is happy with the schedule and grateful for your quick response. This date will make it easy for me to be on hand to make the introductions, as I've been away for a long time and need to get back home for the holiday. It is an easy drive down to the ranch, so if there are no changes, I will see you there. If you need anything at all, you should call me."

"OK, we will proceed. I will make our flight plans, and there will be no changes. That would be impossible; everyone is booked to the minute," Korsikov assured him.

"If you could let me know your ETAs and how many people will be coming, then we can make sure your needs will be met, and the chef can prepare what should be a memorable feast."

"All right, I will call you after the weekend."

"Thank you. Talk to you then."

Del Mundo picked up on the first ring. "I was about to call you," he said.

"We just confirmed the schedule for the Tuesday before Thanksgiving. They will arrive in two aircraft— one for bankers, the other for our boy, which has me already with a convenient plan of action right at the strip. This date should allow you ample time to cruise and get set up." Nick told him.

"Yes, even a couple of days will be useful. We will begin preparations and be under way by this evening. It may be prudent to leave Smith with you in case of any complications at the tower, technical or otherwise. He can then fly down with you and your boss."

"That is a good idea. Let's do that."

"If we are lucky, he won't be needed here, but if we don't leave him, the chances are good that something will pop up."

"Right. I will have the rabbi send a car to bring him here, and you can let me know when you are under way."

"Roger that."

"We had better tell Helen there will be one more mouth to feed for a few days."

"Wowoof."

Helen had no problem with Smith showing up and said she had met him on an operation and approved of him. This meant no extra drama, which was a relief. The rabbi concurred with the wisdom of this detail. The other advantage was for Nick and Smith to have a chance to plot and scheme and to determine what was technically feasible. This would give them time to construct or order any specialty equipment they might need. With the immediate plan settled, Nick delved into the ranch information and brochure, getting the lay of the land and picturing the pending action and how it would be best staged. Turning on a news channel, he was again shocked to see how many of the president-elect's untruthful statements and outrageous claims every day were becoming normalized after so many repetitions. This environment continued to support the importance of their actions, possibly being the only chance to save the democracy.

These dark thoughts motivated Nick to consider everything and anything, no matter how small, that could undermine their efforts. His thinking was interrupted by del Mundo's call. "Hey, Nick, we are under way, just cleared the moorage. Smith should be at your door any minute. Call if you need, but we will see you in Texas."

"All right, Professor. Bon voyage."

"Thanks, you too."

The back doorbell rang. Mom went to see with Nick on her heels. Smith had two duffels of gear and said, "Hi, Mom. How you? Oh, hi, Nick." Mom was glad to have another friend in the house, a potential advocate for increased Milk-Bone allowances from her partner.

"It is good that we all know each other and can get along in our growing family," Helen said, having met Smith on previous operations.

"Wowoof."

"Which brings us to the question of dinner, and that hour is nearly upon us," Smith said.

"And to think I was happy for a minute, but now there are two Nick-type creatures to deal with, and you are luckier than you know that Mom is here to keep the two crazies from going the rest of the way over the edge."

"Rrwoof."

"There is a fantastic Chinese restaurant around the corner that we have vetted regularly for years. Why don't

I call for one of everything for takeout?" Helen picked up the phone.

"How about just half of everything?" Nick said.

"Like your wit, you mean."

"Suit yourself," was all Nick could manage.

Smith called dibs on gopher duty and was out the door with Mom doing a hangdog act, like she was being left out of a walk. Nick knew her too well to buy that one. "You just thought if you could have gone with Smith, you would get some fortune cookies, didn't you?"

"Rrrr woo."

"That's what I thought."

The Chinese food was as good as advertised, and Mom's kibble was excellent, resulting in a happy, well-fed family.

The weekend passed with exercise walks and gaming the ranch action. Nick took the call from Korsikov reconfirming the date and listing the people in both entourages. He would be bringing his assistant and two security men whom he referred to as "staff." The president would bring his business attorney and two "staff" members. Both aircraft would arrive by 11:00 a.m. and depart before dark. "Hawkins" told the Russian that he would be there Monday night to make sure they would have everything they needed, including the jet-fuel tanker. He would also make sure the chef would prepare a spectacular "ranch lunch" that they would find memorable. This all sounded good, and they looked forward to meeting in a week.

Checking in with Corbone, Nick was told that there had been no further calls from the tenant and that he doubted there would be any. If there were any questions, he was certain that he could find a reason to stall. With a promise of a call if anything came up, he thanked Corbone, hung up, and dialed the rabbi. Clicks, buzzes, and then, "Hi, Nick, how are you coming along?"

"Fine, thanks. Smith and I have been scheming all weekend and have a plan in the works. Korsikov reconfirmed and provided lists of the entourage. Del Mundo and the *Bubble* have been sailing and will be in the gulf in two more days. We will need a ride tomorrow or the day after for Smith, Mom, and me, directly to the ranch if possible."

"Yes, good. I will see where your ride is and give you an itinerary. You might be interested to know that your giant is recovering from broken hands and memory loss. He is also here illegally and worried, wanting to make a deal. We can keep him on ice indefinitely talking about his options. I will call you soon."

Nick could almost chuckle about the big tough guy looking for a way out until he remembered how close their encounter had been to having a different result.

During a dinner of top sirloins, baked potatoes, artichokes, and a tossed salad, Nick's phone had the rabbi calling. "Hey, Nick, how is dinner? Am I interrupting?"

"Of course. What's up?"

"You three will be picked up by the van at eleven o'clock tomorrow morning for your luncheon flight to the ranch, if that is convenient."

"Let me think about it. Yes, that will be fine."

"Good. Have a nice ride. Please call me when you arrive."

"Roger, out."

Finishing the tasty dinner, Nick thought about leaving Helen's company the next day and knew he would miss her sarcastic good spirits—something to think about, a new emotion to put on a shelf while he focused on the important mission. With a good night's sleep, a morning exercise walk with his partner, and then a light breakfast of oatmeal, fruit, toast, and coffee, he, along with his team, was packed and ready for the van, which arrived precisely at 11:00 a.m. After loading their gear and getting a lingering hug from Helen, they were off to a private aviation facility where the *Citation* waited, fueled and ready. The gear stowed, they were in and belted, wheels up in minutes. The "luncheon" part of the flight was either a ham-and-cheese or chicken-salad sandwich, chips, and bottled water. Mom had two Milk-Bones and was content. The flight was smooth, the naps good, and four hours later they touched down at the ranch.

They were met by Hawkins's "friend," the owner, Jimmy Ray Barnes, a decorated army veteran in his sixties who had worked with del Mundo over the years on a variety of projects. A lean, weathered-looking cowboy of average height, with gray hair and bright-blue eyes, Barnes appeared authentic in jeans, plaid shirt, fancy boots, and a straw hat. "Welcome to the ranch, and who is this lovely lady?" he asked, letting Mom have a sniff of his hand and a quick lick. "This is going to be fun. When del Mundo outlined this event, I was thrilled to be in a position to help stop this traitorous clown in his tracks. I have been disgusted and upset for a year now, and this part of the country has been completely suckered in. I have built this place up for years and am glad to put it to use to help defend our democracy. I hope you have a good plan."

"It is nice to meet you, sir, and thanks for pitching in," Nick said.

"First thing, son, drop the 'sir.' I go by Jimmy Ray. I owe everything to this country and will be damned if I can sit by and let a Russian thug and a lying con man steal it out from under us."

"Jimmy Ray, we are all on the same page here, and although we were a little slow out of the gate, we are in motion and as determined as you. Our action here should blunt the attack and put us in front of their agenda instead of running from behind, as has been the case."

"Well, giddyup go, let me show y'all around, and pardon me, sir, I didn't get your name," he said, stretching out his hand to Smith.

"Smith. Drop the 'sir,' please. It's real nice to meet you."

"Likewise. So where is that rascal del Mundo?"

"He should be in the gulf by now," Smith said.

"Is he still floating around on that old tin can?"

"Yes, but she has gone through multiple refits and now is a megayacht named *Bubble*," Nick said.

"And are we a good girl and glad to be out of that little plane?" Jimmy Ray scratched Mom's ears.

"Rrrrruf."

"She is already talking to you, Jimmy Ray. I think you have a new friend."

"Well, it is certainly mutual. As you might have noticed, I am an animal lover and practice my animal husbandry by preventing any one species from overpopulating at the expense of the others. We occasionally even make a buck or two for our efforts."

"Why wouldn't you?" Nick said.

"Would you like to take a tour?"

"Sure."

"Come on," said Jimmy Ray, walking to a large hangar. They followed and got into a five-seat all-terrain vehicle. Jimmy Ray buzzed open a door, and they were out the back side of the building and in fifty yards running forty miles an hour on a dirt road through thickly wooded hills and rock formations around a fast-running mountain stream. The terrain became tighter, and they slowed to a fast-walking pace, following the trail across a dry creek bed and then up and through a boulder field. At the top of a rise, Jimmy Ray stopped, and they saw a meadow ahead with a serious-looking steel fence. "That is the edge of the big game preserve. This trail runs outside the fence on the entire perimeter, spanning the streams, which have underwater posts to prevent any large-animal escape. We use the newest wildlife-management programs designed by the university scientists and limit the number of each species culled so our populations can remain neutral. Deer and elk make up the most kills due to their large herd size and nonendangered-species status. The more exotic game kills are very limited, and, yes, those folks pay a bit more for their experience."

"That sounds like a very positive concept," Nick said.

"Yes, thank you. We think so, and all the studies have shown our animals to be healthier and more sustainable than all the zoos and many natural settings," Jimmy Ray said proudly.

"You have done an admirable job of combining two opposing opinions of animal care in a beautiful setting. The trophy hunters are satisfied, while quotas and species protection are honored and achieved. I would bet that these considerations are lost on the would-be buyers, whose only concern is the laundering of their ill-gotten cash."

"I think you are correct, Nick, and that fact is part of my decision to allow this resource to be the bait to trap these criminals and help protect our democracy."

"Your playacting should be simple enough for this deal, Jimmy Ray. We have represented you as a person anticipating family issues leading to legal action and wanting to avoid this trouble at any cost, even the cost of selling your project at a loss. I doubt you will be questioned about details, and if you are, you can say that it is a private matter too difficult to discuss. They don't care about your or anyone else's problems, only how they can be used for their advantage," Nick said.

"This will be no problem, and I will speak as little as possible, playing the reluctant seller. They are interested in closing the deal, washing their money, and running, and would not like to waste time talking with me. This will be fun. This was the mini tour. Let's get back to the resort so you can settle in. I think you will like our cabins."

The "cabin" that they would occupy was more like a three-bedroom bungalow at an exclusive hotel with log walls and a stone fireplace. All bedrooms were suites, and there were a fully equipped kitchen with high-end appliances, a large dining room, and a spacious living room. All rooms had picture windows with wilderness views. Nick was impressed and told Jimmy Ray

"We just want our guests to be comfortable," Jimmy Ray said modestly.

After an early supper of game stew that was unusual and tasty, the three returned to the cabin. Nick spread out his notes on the desk in the living room and went to work. Smith set up his electronic gear for checking. Mom, always working, crunched her kibble, keeping an eye on Nick and Smith.

Nick called del Mundo, who said the *Bubble* would be in Trinity Bay the next day, anchoring at the northern end, a short launch ride to get close to the ranch, well within range of the electronics. Next, he called the rabbi, who after the clicks and buzzes asked Nick how the ranch looked.

"Quite a place, and Jimmy Ray is a real patriot, a very good guy. Mom took to him right away. It was mutual, and you know that is always a good sign. He knows his role, will play it well, and is all in support of the plan, glad to be part of stopping the theft of our country. To say he is motivated is an understatement."

"He has always been a strong patriot, never shying away from putting it all on the line. Are you coming along with your plan?"

"Yes, the two different planes for our boy and the Russians will play nicely, making the divide-and-conquer more workable." Nick then explained the plan, and the rabbi approved and said he would put his people on ready status. Nick told him that del Mundo was on schedule and would be in the area the next day. The rabbi said they should talk again then and hung up.

The morning brought a scenic run around the preserve trail and then a western omelet in the dining hall for Nick and Smith, and kibble for Mom. Smith had all his gadgets serviced, wiped down, and ready. Nick showered and dressed and worked on his notes, fine-tuning the plan when del Mundo called.

"Good morning, Nick. We are anchored in Trinity Bay near the Lost River. Jones and Black are launching the boat and will see how far upstream toward the ranch they can get. When they have gone as far as possible in the boat, they will call you with their position, and you can pick them up."

"Good. Jimmy Ray has used the holiday as a reason for closing the ranch to guests, and he has a fleet of trucks, Jeeps, and all-terrain vehicles and has offered the use of whatever we need. When you call with the position, he will know which vehicle is best, and I will pick them up."

"OK, talk to you soon."

When Jones and Black called with their coordinates, Jimmy Ray said they were only ten to fifteen miles away and that Nick could take a Jeep Wrangler to pick them up, and he gave him directions. Smith volunteered for gopher duty again and found the dirt roads good. He was shortly back at the ranch with the crew and gear. Mom greeted them for lots of scratches and moaned, happy to see old friends. They went to the main lodge to meet Jimmy Ray, who had laid out a delicious barbecue lunch of buffalo burgers, baked beans, and coleslaw.

After lunch, they went to work, first in the meeting room where all the paperwork, wire transfers, and signing would take place. They installed well-hidden mini-cameras and mini-microphones in the beams, walls, and furniture. Nick reminded them that there would be four principals—the two bankers, the president-elect, and his attorney—and four security people in the target group. Jimmy Ray showed them to a large basement storeroom where they could set up the command center with the screens, speakers, and recording equipment. The space had desks and chairs, a refrigerator, and a bathroom, so it would be a self-contained work space for the day. He asked if they needed a cabin, but since it was to be a one-day operation, a cabin was not necessary. They would commute to the *Bubble* to sync the onboard equipment to the ranch devices. Jimmy Ray told them to take the Jeep and leave it where they had moored the rigid inflatable boat, and he would see them in the morning. After installing the equipment, they had a light supper, thanked the modest host for the ground support and everything else, and motored away on the dirt road, leaving Smith to fine-tune his gadgets.

Black and Jones arrived early and with Smith completed the equipment installations and testing until they were satisfied that all systems were go. They all gathered for another exotic barbecue lunch. Nick called the rabbi to discuss his plan; after a few minor adjustments, they both felt it was good. The rabbi said he would have Treasury agents on-site and ready at dawn. They were to be out of sight in a remote cabin in the woods until they were needed for the action. Everything was set, and everyone would be in position early, ready for the target's arrival.

Then it was Tuesday, cloudy and cool, and the show was about to begin. Smith, Jones, and Black were bunkered in the storage room with their equipment, all systems go. They were dressed in tactical gear, ready for any action required. The Treasury people were in their cabin, completely out of sight, off the beaten path. They would be unknown and undisturbed until time to act. Mom would keep the crew company in the basement monitoring room, unseen and unheard, joining Nick after the signing and banking activity, when Nick and his team would be in black tactical gear, come out and around through the woods to the back of the hangar, and join the Treasury team, all unseen and poised for action. Jimmy Ray had his attorney with him along with Carl, his ranch manager, a strapping cowboy type who would help with the short tour for the buyers.

The first plane to arrive was the president-elect with his attorney and two security men. Along with the pilots, they were all shown in to the well-appointed lounge for coffee and soft drinks to await Korsikov's arrival. After fifteen minutes, they heard radio contact. The second airplane touched down and taxied to the flight center, where Korsikov, his assistant, his two security men, and pilots joined the group in the lounge. "Hawkins" introduced them all to his friend, Jimmy Ray, who shook hands around and welcomed them all.

"I thought we would begin with a tour of the property. My ranch hand, Carl, will escort us and be able to answer any questions you may have, as can I. We can load into the all-terrain vehicles to get a look at the land and then come back to the main ranch house for lunch and business. The pilots can rest here in the lounge and have their lunch while we do our business. The steward here will take good care of them, and there are recliners if they would like a nap. We are accomplishing a lot here in a short time, so if we are ready, let's go."

All except "Hawkins" piled into the ATVs; he said his injuries from a fall at home would not permit a trail ride, though it wouldn't be dangerous. They were off on a longer perimeter tour than Nick's had been, the plan being for the bumps and dust through the wooded hilly terrain producing an interesting but tiring ride. The wild property and occasional sightings of nonindigenous animals was captivating, as was being belted into a bouncing ATV. The chilly, overcast day contributed to the discomfort, and the strategy was effective. When they arrived at the main lodge, the shaky legs that climbed out of the dusty wagons had Nick biting back a smile. Jimmy Ray just carried on enthusiastically, telling the ranch story while lamenting his need to sell.

"Let's have a special ranch lunch and then take care of our business with full bellies," said Jimmy Ray, leading the group inside. All from the tour readily agreed with this plan and were grateful to be in the warm lodge with a crackling blaze in the gigantic stone fireplace. The lunch was impressive: bear stew, caribou steaks, baked potatoes, mixed vegetables, and freshly baked dinner rolls. The Russians had vodka and beers, the president-elect and his attorney Diet Coke.

After a lengthy feast with some polite storytelling, it was business time. The stack of boilerplate paper was thick, and the attorneys were back and forth, proving their importance, excruciatingly slow. Finally, with the work completed to everybody's satisfaction and signed, the funding transfers began with the entire purchase amount being wired from the Russian bank to Jimmy Ray's account in his Houston bank. This was conducted under the supervision of the attorneys. When Jimmy Ray's man was satisfied that the funds were received and available, the deed was signed over to the president-elect's real estate company with the Russian bank named as lien holder. After the seemingly never-ending process, all parties were relieved that the ordeal was finally over—or so they thought.

The Russians and Jimmy Ray had a few vodka toasts and loaded into the ATVs for the short ride to the airfield. "Hawkins" begged off, saying he was worn out and hurting and needed to rest. With the group slowly motoring off, Nick hustled to change into tactical gear with mask in the storeroom, where Mom greeted him happily with moans, leaning into him for the scratches. "Did you miss me all morning, girl?"

"Rrwoof."

"You are a good girl," he said with the Milk-Bone. "Did the equipment work, or do we need to bring everyone back for a rerun?" he asked Smith.

"We have every move, blink, and utterance on video and audio with good pictures and sound."

"Excellent. Now comes the fun part." They put on the masks and hustled down the path through the woods to the back of the hangar, where they joined the Treasury crew concealed between the heating and mechanical sheds.

As planned, the president-elect's plane was first in line, and he and his group said their good-byes and boarded. With all systems go and clearance from the small tower, they were wheels up and gone. The ground crew now had the Russian plane out and in position, and the bankers said their farewells and went out to board.

At this signal, the fuel truck stopped in front of the plane, and the Treasury agents came around the building, joined by Smith and Jones while Nick and Mom crept around to the far side of the plane, unseen. The Treasury men closed in, with the leader using a high-volume bullhorn to announce, "We are the United States Treasury Department. Stop where you are." Korsikov scrambled into the plane with his assistant while his security men took position behind the stairs, pulled pistols, and opened fire, hitting one agent as the others ducked for cover.

From the other side of the plane, behind the gunmen, still unseen, Nick and Mom moved quickly. Mom was quicker, racing for the nearest gunner, and did her gun hand crunch and brought him down yelling in pain. The other Russian heard the screams, turned, and tried to line up a shot at the fast-moving Mom, who was vigorously dragging her man around by his useless, empty gun hand. After one wild shot, Nick hit him with a running dive and pulled the gun hand down as he drove his shoulder into the Russian's solar plexus, taking him down. Nick disarmed the Russian and broke his wrist in the process.

The agents and Smith raced up the stairs into the plane to secure the bankers and pilots. The motors were spooled down and off, and the lead Treasury agent announced that they were all under arrest on suspicion of international money laundering. They were shocked and confused as they were read their rights and cuffed and then all bundled into the Treasury van, which had pulled in out of sight behind the hangar. They were driven away, and their plane was towed back into the hangar.

A refreshing quiet engulfed the ranch. The agent who went down was lucky that the bullet had hit his torso, which was protected by his body armor. He would be sore with a severe bruise but knew how fortunate he was to have sustained no serious or fatal injuries.

They regrouped in the main lodge for the after-action assessment. Nick called the rabbi, who picked up quickly. "Nick, you are able to call. Can I deduce that the operation was successful?"

"Yes, sir. We had one Treasury man take a bullet in his vest, but other than bruising and possibly a cracked rib, he will be fine. The timing was perfect with the president-elect airborne and out of sight before the action, with no idea what was transpiring. The entire Russian group—bankers, security staff, and pilots—are in the van, cuffed, and traveling to the Treasury Department's holding facility in Houston. They were read their rights, charges are being written, funds were seized, and the title transfer was voided. The surveillance equipment performed flawlessly, so we have ironclad recorded evidence of the event."

"Congratulations, and good work by all, including Jimmy Ray. It will be interesting to monitor the president-elect's reactions when he hears what happened. The Russians will see him as the informant who set them up, which will put an end to that cozy relationship. His options have just been reduced to one: following our instructions. There will be no going back to the Russians for him; that play is over. One question is how much this will trigger them to release any compromising material of him they may have and how many loans they will call due, potentially bankrupting his projects. On the other hand, they could remain quiet, not wanting to implicate themselves in other prosecutable activities. Either way, there will be tremendous fallout, when the news breaks."

"Yes, and we could order him to be more and more destructive to the point that Congress will have to impeach," Nick said.

"That is certainly an option now," said the rabbi. "We have a great amount of analyzing and interpreting to do before any announcements are released, but the options at this point are all ours. This will be a long-term fight, but we have the funds, Jimmy Ray still has his beloved ranch regardless of how much, if any, of the story is made public. The one result, regardless of what happens next, is that the Russians will believe that their boy burned them, which is not a healthy place to be even if you have won an election."

Chapter 14

●　　●　　●

THE RACE CONVERGES, FINALE

While the Russians were cuffed in the Treasury van awaiting transport, Nick, Mom, and Jimmy Ray had hustled back to the main lodge, where Nick and Mom quickly changed into the Hawkins persona costumes. As the van with the Russians drove by the lodge, they observed Hawkins, Jimmy Ray, and the ranch manager being led out in handcuffs to a second Treasury van that followed. When the first van was out of sight, they made a U-turn and returned to the ranch, where the three got out, joking that they had the shortest arrest ever by the Treasury Department. Following their plan, Jimmy Ray and the ranch manager would stay inside, out of sight for a time, to reinforce the arrest story. Nick and Mom were picked up that night and flown back to his island to stay out of sight, preserving the arrest story. The *Bubble* hauled anchor and took a slow cruise back to New York to its moorage.

After a relaxing break on his island, fishing and training with Mom, and a surprise visit from Helen, talking and at last loving together in the off-duty setting, Nick got a call from the rabbi. "Hi, Nick, are you guys all rested up and relaxed?"

"Yes, thanks, and so is Mom."

"Woof."

"Good. Now comes the interesting part. Next week, the taxi will collect all three of you for your luncheon flight to New York."

"Interesting?" Nick asked.

"Interesting, yes, and more. We need to ramp up the pressure before the inauguration. We have information now that most of the campaign crew omitted Russian contacts from their security-clearance declarations. The web grows with each new detail. You and Jimmy Ray will want the president-elect to believe that you were being set up along with the Russians."

"I still like it, giving him some lesser antagonists than the lethal Russians, whose reaction is probably very worrisome to him. He is backed into a corner, with the committee his only way out."

"Correct. I will arrange your transportation, and we can talk when you are all back in the safe house. How is Helen?"

"Ornery as usual."

"A good match."

Nick could not argue with the rabbi's assessment, though for now he was not talking.

All too soon, the vacation was over, and they were back in the safe house. The press was now reporting the arrest of Russian nationals along with unidentified American citizens in a money-laundering scheme.

"We can hold the Russians for a while, but it is logical that US citizens have bailed out," the rabbi said as he began the call. "For you to be angry and accusatory will be natural. You have been instructed to have no contact with coconspirators, but this does not include the president-elect, who has not been charged."

"Yes, Hawkins and his friend, Jimmy Ray, are royally pissed off, Jimmy Ray near psychotic with the ranch now tied up and still facing the family problems," Nick said. "It is time to go door knocking."

"Exactly. We need constant pressure, partly to keep him occupied with only limited time to further weaken the country, so it's more tower duty for you and your boss."

"I will call Williams, who may not know who the news stories involve."

"Like I said, interesting."

"But not funny."

"You got it."

After a lunch of lobster bisque, salad, and fresh rolls, with kibble for Mom, Nick got to work. His first call was to Corbone. "Hello, Mr. Corbone. Neil Miller here. How are you and your tower?"

"Hi, Mr. Miller. Good to hear from you. The building is fine with not a word about the elevator problem. I just saw a news story about some Russian money-laundering scheme, with some mention of names that were in our guest log. What is that all about?"

"Well, of course, officially, I know nothing, but some bankers' activities are troubling."

Corbone laughed. "That answer is what I expected, but I am glad that you are OK."

"Yes, we try to keep our heads above water. It is good that your tenants are too preoccupied to do more back-tracking. I would be surprised if you hear any more from them. Thank you again, and please call if you do hear from them again. Take care."

"You too. Good-bye."

Next, Nick checked in with del Mundo, who reported having a leisurely cruise through the Bahamas and expected to be on station by late evening.

He then called Williams, who sounded surprised to hear from Hawkins, which told Nick that he had some knowledge of the ranch drama.

"Hello, Mr. Hawkins, are you OK? I have been wondering about you."

"OK is probably a stretch. I am back in town and would like to meet with you and the president-elect for a brief conversation to clear up a few things."

Williams hesitated and then said, "I will check schedules and let you know a good time."

"Hopefully soon. I don't know what you have heard, but I can assure you that the situation is critical, so sooner is better for all concerned."

"I will start on this immediately and let you know what our schedules permit."

"Immediately is a good word. I will await your call." To Mom, he said, "That was a lot of phone time, girl. Do you think we should have a walk?"

"Wowoof."

"That's what I thought. Let's go."

After a fast run/walk with training, they were back home for the sweep, Helen sounds, and Milk-Bone. Nick showered and went downstairs for dinner. Helen did not ask Nick for menu approval but just informed him what they would have—a new procedure corresponding with their new intimacy. Nick was happy but nervous about their growing relationship, as probably was Helen. They enjoyed a Caesar salad, grilled snapper, and vegetables, Mom her kibble. Their only decision after dinner was whether to sleep upstairs or down.

Next morning, there was oatmeal, toast, fruit, and coffee, and then the morning walk in costume, back home for the sweep, Helen sounds, and shower, interrupted by the phone.

"Good morning, Mr. Hawkins. Gene Williams here. I could meet with you this afternoon with the head of the transition team. The president-elect is very busy with multiple interviews of prospective appointees, really a constant stream, so he may not be able to join us himself."

"I understand he is busy, but my friend and I have also been very busy dealing with our arrests by the Treasury Department. Did you say two o'clock in the lobby bar meeting room?"

"Yes, that will be fine," Williams replied hesitantly.

"See you then."

Del Mundo then checked in. The *Bubble* was back on station, all electronics up and running, including the minicameras and sound from the penthouse, which were linked up with the rabbi and the committee. Next came the ring, clicks, and buzzes, and the rabbi was speaking. "Hey, Nick, what is your status?"

"I have spoken with Corbone. No further questions about elevators, and our devices remain intact and functional. I spoke with Williams yesterday, requesting a meeting with him and the president-elect, who he said is interviewing nonstop and probably not able to meet. He called back earlier, and we will meet this afternoon with the transition manager. I laid into him about our arrest, and I expect this meeting will be uncomfortable."

"Good. It is time to ratchet up the pressure, and the committee 'voice' will be talking with our boy after your meeting."

"OK, I will fill you in afterward."

A quick lunch, and Nick and Mom took the in-costume slow walk to the tower, which was a beehive of activity, with people moving through the lobby and the elevators running nonstop.

"Hello, Mr. Hawkins. Good to see you." Williams, accompanied by another man, greeted him at the door.

"I hope you have some answers for me," said Nick, shaking the outstretched hand after a long pause.

"Mr. Hawkins, I would like you to meet Pete Edwards, who is heading up the transition team. They shook hands and sat at the table, under which the invisible Mom had installed herself.

"Let's not waste time on banalities," Nick said. "My friend Jimmy Ray and I were arrested along with Russian bankers and aides in a money-laundering conspiracy operation after the president-elect left the ranch. The ranch has been seized, the purchase funds confiscated, and we were released on bond after being held for days. Jimmy Ray is out everything, still facing his personal problems and concerned for the welfare of the animals. So far, we have heard nothing about the president-elect, and my friends and family are being hurt badly after contributing to the campaign through the PAC. We want to know what is going on. Was he forced into setting everyone up to avoid FBI charges of collusion or obstruction involving the Russian election interference? What the hell is going on with the bankers, ranch owners, and manager, as well as myself arrested with funds and properties seized while the president-elect just goes about preparing for his inauguration as if there is nothing wrong? We want some answers, and we want them now, and don't insult me by telling me to take it easy."

Visibly shaken, Williams said he knew only what he saw on the news, which provided few details. Nick was told that the president-elect was too busy for this meeting and that all questions would be referred to his attorney.

"Well, that's just peachy. He didn't need his attorney and was not too busy to take our money. The very least he could do is to give us some explanation. We are hardworking Americans and will not stand for being cannon fodder for some nefarious schemes. I realize, Mr. Williams, that you are only the messenger, so you need to deliver the message to your boss and his attorneys that they will not get away with damaging us so callously. I am leaving now, but we will not go away."

With that said, Nick and the invisible Mom walked slowly out of the room and out of the building. On the sidewalk down the street, Nick told Mom, "Sorry, girl, to put you on alert with my anger act, but it was part of the show and did feel good to let off some steam."

"Rruff."

There were no followers on their usual sidetracking slow walk home. After the sweep, Helen sounds, and Milk-Bone, Nick picked up the phone as the rabbi's clicks and buzzes started.

"Hey, Nick, you really stirred them up with your little meeting. We have been listening to our boy banging around, yelling, and breaking things. Your tirade must have been impressive. Edwards and Williams are real excited, asking about the ranch and the Russians, relaying your questions and frustrations. The only answers they are hearing are not answers, which sounds unacceptable to them. They are, in effect, adding to the pressure for us. I will be making the committee call shortly, so after your meeting, our message will be even more impactful. We can talk later." Click.

Helen had gone to the Chinese restaurant for takeout, and they had a good feast. Then the rabbi called again. "You really stirred them up. Listen to this," he said, keying in the recorded committee call.

"The Russians and Americans all think you set them up to avoid your prosecution for conspiring to rig the election. Protecting you from both will be very difficult, but our ability to do so appears to be your only survival option. Think very carefully and do not trust or talk about this to any advisers, some of whom are compromised. We will permit your inauguration, after which you must follow our instructions to the letter. If you ignore or defy us, we will take immediate action, which will be disastrous for you. Did you really think that we would allow you to do this ranch deal with your Russian banker friends whom we had been surveilling for many months?

Do you know how they deal with those who oppose them? They now believe you set them up to save your own skin from the FBI. After you are sworn in, for your protection, we will instruct you to take actions that favor their interests, though whether they are convinced of your loyalty to them is an open question. We are offering the only path for your survival. This will probably not be a smooth ride, but with your cooperation, you can ride out the bumps. We are your only chance, and we need to compare notes in forty-eight hours. You will hear from us then." Click.

"How did that sound?" the rabbi asked.

"Pretty good. Even an egomaniac can see he is boxed in," Nick said. "I like the ominous-sounding voice disguise."

"We think that is a nice touch. We will be monitoring the penthouse, and two days will give us time to make sure he is playing ball."

"As you told him, he has no other option."

"He is in a corner and is an impulsive person, but he will see that for now he has no other choice. We will have you and del Mundo stay in place through the inauguration and then relocate to DC to stay on top of the action. I will be in touch."

The next month was largely uneventful for the team, a quiet holiday season punctuated with more revelations of campaign contacts with Russians not listed on their security-clearance forms. There were in this time no releases of tax returns nor any movement by the president-elect to separate from personal business dealings. Not only were there no blind trusts, but there were also blatant US concessions to foreign countries bartered for personal-business windfalls, including family members' billion-dollar perks. Then came the inauguration, with the historically small crowds being declared by the new president to be the biggest ever, even showing pictures of previous inauguration crowds claimed as his own.

The *Bubble* moved from New York to DC, berthing at the Navy Yard, partially hidden between two navy vessels, arrangements made by the rabbi. Nick, Helen, and Mom were moved by van to a Georgetown safe house and easily found their usual routine of the early-morning walk with Mom, some all in costume. The other days involved backpack costume changes in a park or underground garage, a fast run by the river, and the change back to Hawkins and service dog, and then home. The dining menu varied, but Helen's sharp humor and cynical barbs did not. The effect on the change in the relationship was rib tickling to Nick, with his unstoppable grin earning him even more abuse. Mom watched the whole thing with glee, anticipating more Milk-Bones in her future.

Much of the day was occupied with monitoring news and intel from all US sources as well as most international reports. The satellite links routed to the safe house were the same as del Mundo's capabilities on the *Bubble*, with some exceptions, including the lack of a large technical staff. The rabbi had confirmed on schedule the new president's unhappy acceptance of the committee's terms and conditions. The team was of unanimous approval of the committee's scheme as the only chance to root out all Russian operatives and their treasonous US citizen coconspirators. Even so, watching a new step, seemingly every hour, taken by the president and his minions to undo progress and damage the nation was unsettling to the point of sickening. They were "deconstructing the administrative state"—the stated goal of the president's right-wing chief adviser. The damage would be irreversible, a democracy turned through an oligarchy into an autocracy. The Russian agenda was a historically proven tactic and advancing too rapidly to be stopped by more traditional means. The destructive parade was gaining strength, and as the rabbi and del Mundo had put it, "The only way to stop or turn a parade is to be in the lead of it."

For a calculated period, the committee would have the new president out-Russian the Russians, putting the committee in front of the parade. He would be blatant and clumsy where the Russians would be cunning and secretive. With the committee leading, the president would push the activity to a point where the con man lies and distractions would become too obvious, the great personal damage to many people too great to be tolerated. People would wake up and rise up, seething mad about themselves and their nation being played. Many calls for impeachments and accountability would follow.

A messy process would be in store, but not as disastrous as the present path remaining unchecked until too late.

The weeks passed, each bringing more backward steps, reversing recent progress, along with more revelations of wrongdoing and influence peddling. There was a complete disdain and ignoring of laws and traditions, and the establishment of a royal family immune to all laws was more emboldened every day. The race was on. Would the dam break with the people demanding impeachments and removal of Russian-collaborating officials before the press was muffled and military and National Guard units mobilized under martial law to suppress all opposition, discarding the Constitution and rule of law? The situation was that serious to the team and to the majority of US citizens. A breaking point was imminent.

Following the committee's directions, the new president took step after step to diminish the standing of the United States in the world and antagonize its strongest allies while praising dictators around the world. Both its northern and southern neighbors were alienated by ridiculous actions and threats, while European friends were damaged by reneging on trade and climate agreements. The praises and welcoming to the White House of foreign dictators were galling, including the security guards of a Turkish dictator assaulting US citizens who were protesting, all within view of the Capitol, with no concern from Republican lawmakers, sending the signal that future suppression would go unchallenged.

Added to this mix was the failed attempt to have the FBI director drop an investigation, followed by his firing. Democratic candidates for office were subjected to death threats. For Nick and the watching team, the nonstop absurdities and outright lies dominating the news were escalating, and they saw the breaking point rapidly approaching.

The day came in early summer when Nick's phone rang, buzzed, and clicked. "Nick, good morning," the rabbi said. "We will be hearing news released later today that puts the president and associates directly involved with the Russian election interference and their family businesses profiting from their government access. To have these acts unquestionably documented will be the last straw. When these stories broadcast later, most citizens will break from this president and his enablers. Millions of Americans will take to the streets demanding impeachments or more. This will be the real test for the president. Will he stay with our plan or make a last-minute power grab to attempt the coup, which has been the Russian goal all along? If he takes this course, then we will have a revolution with loyalists fighting to save the democracy. We have been girding our strength, preparing many generals, sheriffs, Secret Service agents, police, and National Guard units for an upcoming attempted coup. We are confident that we have the numbers and people in place to thwart the attack. It will be a dicey situation with you,

Mom, and del Mundo's crew needed in the middle of the action.

"The scope of the conspiracy involves so many players that we foresee multiple impeachments including the president, vice president, and many congressmen and officials. This president is untrustworthy and unpredictable, so we must be prepared for this last-minute attempt to steal the government. While he technically commands military and National Guard units, we have been involved with many of these commanders and believe enough are loyal patriots who will reject his orders. We have also discovered a subplot of Russians disguising themselves as National Guardsmen to get close to the president and assassinate him if the coup is failing. We cannot allow the coup to succeed, nor can we allow the Russians to kill the president, who must be tried in a court of law, not martyred. It seems like we have been fiddling while the fire grows, but by tonight our Capitol could resemble a war zone. We have had the nervous calm; now comes the storm."

"That was a mouthful." Nick said. "Do you think these revelations are the tipping point and today is D day?"

"Yes, this new information will be so outrageous that calls for impeachment will be immediate, and the only escape is for the president and his cohorts to attempt to seize control. I wish I were sure this was not possible, but anything is possible with this person, so be ready. It's all coming to a head."

"That is a dire possibility, but we stand ready."

"Good. We will stay in close touch."

Next, del Mundo checked in. "Did you hear from the rabbi?"

"Yes, and he said your crew was ready to join the party."

"Smith and Jones have taken the launch, will dock nearby, and will be at your door soon. Black will remain on board to man the electronics, watch the news and satellite feeds, and be ready."

"Roger, out."

Smith and Jones arrived at the safe house a few minutes later. After giving greetings to Nick and Helen and scratches for Mom, Smith dug a packet from his duffel of Secret Service special agent identification passes for all four, including Mom, which would allow access to all parts of the White House. He also brought Secret Service jackets for the three and a logo Secret Service vest for Mom with Velcro-sealed pockets for extra clips, zip ties, and other gear, including hooded masks to protect their identities. The rabbi had sent these items to the *Bubble*.

"Nice to see you sailors all set to go," Nick said.

"You too," said Smith. "Del Mundo said that when the broadcasts begin, we should take positions in the White House. A van will be outside waiting in five minutes."

"I think we could use some energy bars and protein shakes before the action," Nick said.

"Rruff."

"Yes, Mom, and some protein kibble for you and Milk-Bones in the vest for the road."

"Wowoof."

They watched the screens for a half hour of normal rehashing of who said what, and then the breaking-news alarms announced the evidence that proved collusion by most campaign staff as well as many Congress members and officials of various departments of the new administration. They were shocked at the depth of the conspiracy, even after all they had known.

"It has begun; let's go," Nick said. They piled into the waiting van to the White House.

The government stickers on the van got them to the service entrance, where the identification documents gave them entry to the building. The news reports had spread quickly, and crowds were building in the streets. Many protesters carried signs, and all were angry and calling for impeachment. These groups were opposed by Nazi and Confederate-flag-waving skinheads and other right-wing supporters of the president, all armed to the teeth. Minute by minute, the scene grew more tense, with isolated skirmishes breaking out.

Nick and Mom were watching from a rooftop perch while Smith and Jones were positioned inside to watch the Oval Office and president's quarters. The crowd was growing rapidly and would soon number in the hundreds of thousands. When an explosion set by Russians and the president's supporters leveled a vacant building blocks away, the president immediately declared martial law. The crowd went from disorderly to rabid. Next, a National Guard unit from a southern state deployed and began arresting protesters. When the pro-impeachment groups saw what was happening, a full-scale riot broke out and turned into a shooting war. The air was filled with smoke, constant gunfire, flash bangs, and tear gas grenades.

Nick and Mom joined Smith and Jones inside, sealing off the office where the president and Secret Service agents had gathered, having not had time to exit to the bunker. Smith and Jones used their electronic bag of tricks to lock the doors, containing the president's group inside. On the streets, the battle grew more intense, with many protesters beaten, cuffed, and hauled away. The violence increased until the White House was under siege with only the fences and US Marine sharpshooters keeping the fighting groups outside the grounds. The battle raged on until a contingent of loyal marines arrived and overwhelmed the phony National Guard unit and the skinheads, shooting the ones firing weapons and disabling and cuffing others, bringing order step by step to the fighting crowds.

A small band of National Guard imposters had breached a back entrance and were swarming toward the Oval Office. Smith and Jones returned fire, stopping some, but were then pinned down behind a hastily built barricade of steel desks and filing cabinets. Nick and Mom fell in behind a handful from this group, who set charges and blew the door to the office. Four of the guard members raced in, not realizing that the man and dog had followed them, obscured by the smoke. They ambushed the back two, Nick taking one down with a rifle butt that nearly took his head off while Mom put one on the floor with jaws clamped on the back of his neck. Neither man moved. As Nick stepped over the body and out of the smoke, he saw the other two confronting the president, yelling at him in Russian. The president had soiled himself, and the Russians had guns pointed at his face when Nick, with no time left, shot them both before they could carry out the execution.

"Y-y-you saved my life. They were going to kill me," the president stammered.

"And you thought they were your allies," Nick said drily. "We believe in the Constitution and the rule of law in our country."

The Russians had killed the Secret Service men in the room, two with the door-breaching explosion. The other three had been shot by the pair who would have executed the president, whom they had never trusted after the ranch sting. One of the fallen agents had been the keeper of the briefcase with the nuclear codes, the "football," so they would need at least one patriotic agent for the next move. Nick's radio squawked with Smith speaking. "We are clear again after the ones you followed blew the door. What's your situation in the office?"

"We are under control, four bad guys down."

Smith squawked again. "The president's private body-guards have collected a handful of corrupted National Guard troops, detonated charges to clear a path, and are coming our way. The loyal Secret Service will be outnumbered."

Nick was glad for the earpiece, or the president would have heard Smith's report and become more embold-ened in his attempted coup.

"Can you and Jones grab two loyal Secret Service men and come in here?" he asked.

"Roger," he said, and they quickly came with two agents.

Nick pulled the group for a quick huddle away from the president and asked for the agent who was cleared to carry the "football," showed him his command creden-tials, and told him what he had in mind. With a "Yes, sir," he took the "football" from his fallen comrade and went to the president's side, standing ready. Next, Nick had the other agent order the Marine One helicopter to the roof. He knew the timing was critical. If the president's private bodyguards with their National Guard helpers got past the remaining Secret Service agents, then the president could complete the coup, protected in the White House by those loyal to him, not the nation.

Nick sent Smith and the other agent to the far side of the building to use massive smoke bombs, flash bangs, and scattered rifle fire to draw the advancing traitors in that direction. He took Jones, Mom, the president, and the agent with the "football" to the rooftop. Waiting for the incoming chopper to touch down, the president recognized his personal bodyguards approaching the building.

Recovering his bluster, he said, "Those are not Russians coming; they are my people. We are staying here." Seeing a last chance to save his coup, he made a lunge for the "football" to threaten them with. Before the agent, following Nick's instructions, did a slip and fall, he pressed the hidden sensor in the handle hinge.

The president threatened, "I'll use this," and grabbed the handle, which triggered a crackling Taser-like jolt that knocked him down, helpless. Marine One landed, and as they loaded the motionless president, the agent, and Mom, who had recovered the "football" on command, Nick called Smith to set more diversionary smoke bombs and hustle up to the roof. It was close, but when they were wheels up and clear, the few remaining Secret Service people stopped fighting, on his signal, and locked themselves in the bunker. There was no further loss of life, and the traitors found only an empty, damaged White House with an impenetrable bunker, and they had no way of knowing whether it held their boss.

Nick had Marine One set down briefly at the river, where Smith and Jones could retrieve the launch to rendezvous at the Navy Yard. When the chopper arrived at the yard, they were met by a contingent of FBI and loyal Secret Service people waiting to escort the president to the secure medical facility along with the agent whom Mom had allowed to take the "football," on Nick's silent command.

Nick told Mom what a good girl she was and got the "Woof" while she crunched her Milk-Bone. The rioting in the streets continued for some time and finally petered out when word of the failed coup spread. With the situation contained, the FBI teams began the process of apprehending the conspirators, including the vice president, members of Congress, and other officials, filling the detention centers overnight (not the privately owned facilities, so no further income for the president's corporate spider web).

A van collected Helen and all the gear and belongings from the safe house to gather in the conference room on board the *Bubble* with Nick, Mom, del Mundo, Merrit, and the entire boat crew. They were soon joined by the rabbi, a senior gentleman of indeterminate age, tall and thin with a hawklike face and gray short hair, wearing lightly tinted wire-rimmed glasses. The rabbi was dressed in a gray silk suit, white shirt, and blue striped tie. He wore a slightly bemused expression, and his calm voice and dark eyes could not mask a sense of relief.

"I wanted to meet all of you in person and thank you for your enormous service to our democracy. This was a close call, too close, and my thanks on behalf of the committee and the nation will be your only medals or acknowledgment. Rest assured, though, that your actions will always be revered by us and that you are now part of our lore. The process that we have begun will require time to complete, but with the many proven treasonous activities of this family and their allies, justice will be served. A failed coup and apprehension of all traitorous conspirators is the outcome, and our democracy will survive, rebuild, and become much stronger and more transparent. Fortunately, we had the HMF." The ones not on the rooftop wondered what that was. "The 'Highly Modified Football' is so classified that the term must never be spoken. I must return to work now and must also disembark before del Mundo has the lines cleared and the *Bubble* sailing to some warm water and sandy beaches to keep you all out of trouble. Again, thank you, and bon voyage."

"Wowowoof."

"And don't be skimping on your boss's Milk-Bones."

"Woof."

ACKNOWLEDGEMENT

The author is very grateful for the incisive guidance from and support of Stanley England-Kerr, which helped make the story what it is.

AUTHOR BIOGRAPHY

Charles K. Spetz was born in Detroit and raised in southwestern Ohio. He studied English and political science at Kent State University before taking on the life of a touring rock musician.

Since then, Spetz has spent time operating a ski racing business in Colorado, working on yachts off the coast of Mexico, and establishing a number of small companies in the United States. Spetz currently resides in the Pacific Northwest.

54197069R00141

Made in the USA
San Bernardino, CA
09 October 2017